ZIGZAG

ZIGZAG

A Nameless Detective Collection

Bill Pronzini

A Tom Doherty Associates Book
New York

ZIGZAG

Copyright © 2016 by the Pronzini-Muller Family Trust

A Forge Book
Published by Tom Doherty Associates, LLC
175 Fifth Avenue
New York, NY 10010

www.tor-forge.com

Forge® is a registered trademark of Tom Doherty Associates, LLC.

The Library of Congress Cataloging-in-Publication Data is available upon request.

ISBN 978-0-7653-8103-3 (hardcover)
ISBN 978-1-4668-7677-4 (e-book)

Our books may be purchased in bulk for promotional, educational, or business use. Please contact your local bookseller or the Macmillan Corporate and Premium Sales Department at 1-800-221-7945, extension 5442, or by e-mail at MacmillanSpecialMarkets@macmillan.com.

First Edition: May 2016

Printed in the United States of America

0 9 8 7 6 5 4 3 2 1

COPYRIGHT ACKNOWLEDGMENTS

For Barbara Lasky,
in fond memory of the Oak Leaf Days

CONTENTS

ZIGZAG
11

GRAPPLIN'
131

NIGHTSCAPE
151

REVENANT
163

ZIGZAG

1

Northern California's Russian River is many things to many different people: water source for sections of Sonoma County and its thriving wine industry, summer resort playground, home to a relatively small and diverse year-round population that includes a once-burgeoning, still-influential LGBT community and culture. The river's main segment is more than a hundred miles long, stretching from its headwaters near Potter Valley to its ocean mouth at Jenner. The American Indian name for it, I'd once been told, was Shabakai—"long snake."

A sleeping snake in the summer and fall, but at this time of year, late February, it has been known to be as deadly as any reptile when it grows bloated enough from heavy winter rains to exceed its thirty-two-foot flood stage. That happens fairly regularly, the most disastrous in recent memory during the winter of 1997–98 when the river had crested at forty-six feet. Three people died, the entire populations of Guerneville and its smaller resort area neighbors, Rio Nido, Monte Rio, and Rio Verdi, had to be evacuated, and scores of low-lying summer and permanent homes had been swamped with water

and/or mud. Most of the residents came back as always—
repairing, rebuilding, replacing lost possessions. River dwellers
are a special breed, modern-day pioneer stock. The harder
they're battered and the greater their losses, the more determined they become.

It had been a while since Northern Californians had had
to deal with chains of storms and constant drenching down-
pours. The severe drought the entire state has suffered through
for four-plus years and counting has seen to that. The previous
year's winter had brought some much-needed rain, enough to
partly fill lakes and reservoirs, streams and wells, but though
one particularly nasty storm had caused flooding, mudslides,
toppled trees, power outages, and several million dollars in
damage, the rainfall totals were not substantial enough to put
an end to the drought. So far this winter's El Niño rains had
started to do the job.

It was raining the afternoon I drove up to the Russian River
from San Francisco, but just the light and misty kind, steady
enough, though, with less than an inch altogether expected
throughout the region. A gloomy day to be out and about on
River Road.

I'd been up here a few times, mainly with Kerry and Emily
on visits to Armstrong Redwoods State Natural Reserve. But
this was a business, not a pleasure, trip. Under normal circumstances, the agency's investigative fieldwork was handled by
Jake Runyon, Alex Chavez, or one of the part-time operatives
Tamara and I employed; in my semiretirement I was usually
deskbound on the two days a week I came into the office. But
we'd lucked into an uncommonly busy period that had everybody available tied up, so rather than bring in someone new
and untried, I'd volunteered to take on the Rio Verdi job myself.

Does me good to get back into the field harness once in a while, like an old but still-durable plowhorse.

The client was an attorney we'd done some work for in the past, the job interviewing witnesses to a two-car automobile accident the previous fall, the object to gather any new information that might be useful to the plaintiff in a civil suit the attorney had filed on behalf of one of the drivers, a San Francisco businessman named Arthur Clements. Clements and his wife had been on River Road, on their way home from visiting relatives, when the other vehicle sped through a stop sign and slammed into the passenger side of their car, causing grievous injuries to Mrs. Clements that confined her to a wheelchair. It was the Clementses' contention that driver number two, David Bishop, a Santa Rosa resident who owned a second home near Rio Verdi, had willfully and negligently run the stop sign, making no attempt to avoid the collision. Bishop was just as adamant that he had been traveling at normal speed on the narrow downhill side road from his cottage when his brakes failed and the collision had therefore been unavoidable. He'd escaped the smashup with nothing more than cuts and bruises.

The official reports and witness statements left some doubt as to which version was the true one. There had been two witnesses, neither of whom was willing or able to make a positive statement either way. Field sobriety tests conducted by the investigating sheriff's and CHP officers had determined that Bishop was not under the influence of either alcohol or drugs, and a subsequent body-shop examination of his vehicle revealed worn brake linings, though no concrete evidence that they'd gone out, so no charges were filed against him. A court judgment in the Clementses' favor was problematical at best, the more so because they were seeking two hundred thousand dollars in punitive damages, but they'd insisted on going ahead anyway. To the attorney's financial benefit, and the agency's and mine, if not to theirs.

I'd gone first to Santa Rosa in an effort to listen to Bishop's account firsthand, but he'd refused to see me. No surprise there. So now here I was at the Russian River, to make an independent examination of the scene of the accident and talk to the witnesses in the slim hope that one or both might be willing to testify in the Clementses' behalf. Not an easy task, but then not all that difficult, either. I'd handled similar investigations dozens of times, more often than not with satisfactory results.

I drove through Guerneville, along the winding stretch to Monte Rio, and then the short distance to Rio Verdi—a misnomer, since the river was not green but silt brown throughout the year. It was not much more than a wide spot in the road, with a handful of buildings: mini-market, service station, funky old saloon with a movie western false front, a couple of uninhabited near derelicts, a propane dealership. The river flowed crookedly behind most of the buildings, all except the market and service station; densely forested slopes of pine and redwood, spotted with typically rustic hidden and half-hidden homes, rose on the opposite side and beyond.

The accident had happened at the intersection with Ridgecrest, a narrow side road that climbed the hillside. The first thing I did was drive up Ridgecrest five hundred yards or so and then come back down, to get a look at its configuration and gauge its steepness. For the last hundred yards to the River Road intersection—I stopped and got out into the chilly drizzle to measure the distance—Ridgecrest was closely bordered by trees with grass-rutted verges not much wider than a man's body. Until you got near the stop sign at the bottom, you couldn't see more than fifty feet or so in either direction along the highway.

Rio Verdi Propane was the last building on the hamlet's west side, close to the intersection. One of the witnesses, George Orcutt, worked there. He'd been out in the narrow lot in front at the time of the accident, and from there, I noted as I swung in, he would've had a more or less unobstructed view of what had taken place.

I parked near a couple of large commercial tanks, entered a cramped and overheated interior. The man behind the counter was forty or so, lanky, fox faced; strands of long caramel-colored hair straggled from beneath a greasy-looking Raiders cap. He squinted at me out of bloodshot eyes, and his hand trembled when he raised it to scratch at a patch of stubble on his chin. Portrait of a man with a bad hangover.

I asked if he was George Orcutt, he said he was, and I told him who I was and why I was there. He looked at the photostat of my license, looked at me as if I were something with claws and scales that had popped up out the netherworld, and then said, scowling, "Lawsuit? Shit, no! I don't want nothing to do with that."

"I'm afraid you don't have any choice. You were a witness to the accident."

"I already told the cops I never seen it clear. I ain't got nothing more to say."

"Just the same, you'll be subpoenaed and you'll have to testify."

"Ah, Christ. Why come around picking on me?"

"No one is picking on you, Mr. Orcutt," I said. "The civil

suit has already been filed and I'm just doing my job, trying to get at the truth of what happened that day."

"Yeah, well, you won't get it from me."

"Just answer a few questions, all right? In your statement you said the vehicle that came down Ridgecrest barreled through the stop sign without slowing. How fast would you say the driver, David Bishop, was going?"

I thought Orcutt was going to put up more argument or else clam up on me, but he did neither. "Hell, I don't know," he said with a twitchy sullenness. "Fast enough to total both cars."

"Faster than he would be if his brakes had been functioning normally?"

Shrug. "I wasn't looking when he come down the hill. Couldn't have seen him clear even if I had been—too many trees and it was foggy that day. Look over there when you leave; see the intersection for yourself."

"Did Mr. Bishop make any attempt to avoid the collision with Mr. Clements' vehicle?"

"Slid mostly sideways right into it, that's all I remember."

"Mostly sideways? The front bumper crushed the passenger side, breaking both of Mrs. Clements' legs and damaging her spine. That type of impact indicates a head-on, not a broadside, collision."

Orcutt had nothing to say to that.

I said, "If you'd been behind the wheel and your brakes went out coming downhill to an intersection at increasing speed, what would you do?"

"Huh? What's it matter what I'd do?"

"I'd appreciate an answer to the question."

A little silence. Then he said, "Slam it into low gear. Yank on the hand brake."

"And then, assuming you saw another vehicle approaching on River Road?"

"Twist the goddamn wheel, if there was enough time."

"What else?"

"What else is there? Go off the road into the trees, kill myself sure by slamming into one of 'em?"

"What about sounding your horn?"

"Yeah. Sure. That's what Bishop said he done."

"Do you remember hearing the horn blow?"

"No. Windy and foggy both, and I wasn't paying no attention until the smash made a hell of a big noise. I told that to the cops, too."

"According to your statement," I reminded him, "you heard a sound that might have been a horn blowing."

"Yeah, might've been. I couldn't be sure."

"How fast would you say Mr. Clements' vehicle was traveling?"

"How fast? I told you, I wasn't paying no attention."

"The speed limit through Rio Verdi is twenty-five. Would you have noticed if he'd been doing forty or better, as Mr. Bishop claims?"

"No. Plenty people don't slow down like they're supposed to."

"David Bishop owns a second home up on Ridgecrest. Do you know him?"

"No."

"Never saw him before the day of the accident?"

"All right, yeah," Orcutt said, "I seen him a few times. He

bought propane refills when he was up here in the summer. But I never said more'n a dozen words to him."

"Have you seen him since the accident?"

"No."

"Sure about that?"

"What, you think he come in here and tried to get me to side with him? Well, he didn't. And I wouldn't of done it if he had." Orcutt ran an unsteady hand over the beard stubble on his chin, making a sandpapery sound. "Listen, mister, that's it; we're done. I got work to do."

Scratch one witness, as far as Arthur Clements' civil suit was concerned. If Orcutt knew anything other than what he'd told the authorities and now me, he was not likely to admit it in court. The old, sorry code of noninvolvement.

I left him to his work and his hangover. I'd have been willing to bet that as soon as he closed business for the day the first place he'd head for was the saloon down the road.

2

The second witness's name was Earline Blunt, a widow in her middle fifties. She called herself, and was known locally as, the Windmill Lady. The reason for that was abundantly evident when I arrived at her roadside home a half mile or so from the scene of the accident. The front and side yards, both shaded by tall pines, were a riot of windmills—little ones not much bigger than pinwheels, large ones taller and broader than garden statuary, and dozens in between. All shapes and sizes, some plain, some painted bright colors and adorned with whimsical illustrations, each—according to the information I had—handmade by the widow Blunt with the assistance of an unmarried daughter she lived with.

The ones on display here served as advertisements as well as yard decorations. Mrs. Blunt made her living, or part of it, selling her creations to various shops along the river and elsewhere in the general area. On this drizzly, windy afternoon, the blades on all of them were spinning merrily and more quietly than you'd expect. Very well constructed, Mrs. Blunt's windmills.

She was home, and much more receptive to me and the

purpose of my visit than George Orcutt had been. Her only reactions were a philosophical sigh and, "I guess I'm not surprised, the way I keep getting called into court for jury duty." She invited me inside, introduced me to her shy and rather homely daughter, Jean, offered me hot tea or coffee—I accepted the latter—and sent Jean off to do the fetching.

We sat in comfortable, overstuffed chairs in a living room brimming with table-size examples of her art. I told her I thought she did wonderful work, and the compliment put her in an even more receptive mood.

"I've always been fascinated by windmills and their history," she said. "Did you know that the first one was invented by a Greek engineer, Heron of Alexandria, in the first century AD?"

"No, I didn't."

"Oh, yes. Others were used as prayer wheels in China and Tibet dating back to the fourth century. Of course, mine have no practical purpose. Some folks consider designing and building miniatures a frivolous pursuit, but others seem to be charmed by them."

The daughter came in with a tray, set it down on the table between her mother and me, and drifted away without a word. Mrs. Blunt abused her cup of tea with three teaspoons of sugar and a splash of what looked like skim milk. She was not quite as overweight as her daughter, but still on the heavy side—a gray-haired, rosy-cheeked woman with a nice dentured smile. Her hands were large and bore the calluses and other marks of her profession. God forbid she should ever develop severe arthritis.

"Well, then," she said as I took a sip of black coffee. "You have questions about the accident, you said?"

"A few, yes."

"I don't know what I can tell you that I didn't tell the investigating officers. But go ahead and ask."

"Let's start by going over exactly what you saw. You were following behind the Clements vehicle when it happened?"

"That's right. I'd just left the Rio Verdi Market."

"Several car lengths behind, according to your statement. About how many would you say?"

"Oh, less than a dozen."

"And you had a clear view of the collision?"

"More or less. It happened very fast."

"As far as you could tell, did Mr. Bishop, the driver on Ridgecrest, take any evasive action when he came through the intersection?"

"Evasive action?"

"Try to swerve out of the way to avoid the collision."

"Well . . . just before he hit the other car, yes."

"Only just before?"

"At the last second."

"He claims he sounded a warning. In your statement you said you couldn't recall hearing his horn blow."

Mrs. Blunt sipped some of her tea, pinky extended like a character in a British drawing room farce, before she answered. "Well, all my windows were closed and it was a windy, foggy day. But I think I would have heard a horn if it had been blowing."

Small points in Arthur Clements' favor. Enough to sway a civil court judge and jury? Probably not.

"Could he have seen the Clements car coming as he neared the intersection?"

"I doubt it. Trees there block your vision, which is why a person should always come slow down the hill."

"Did he seem to be fighting for control of his car, could you tell? The way somebody would if his brakes had gone out and he was trying to use gears or the emergency brake to reduce his speed?"

"That's a hard question to answer. The accident happened so fast, as I said. He might have been, I suppose, but . . . well, the impression I had was of a person going too fast and not paying proper attention."

"But you can't be sure?"

"No. It was just an impression." Her jaw firmed and she added deprecatingly, "I'm very aware of distracted drivers these days. The ones who talk or text on their cell phones are a menace. The fines for that kind of carelessness ought to be much larger than they are."

I agreed completely. Stiffer fines was the only way to reduce the number of idiots who believe they can safely do one or two other things while operating a couple thousand pounds of potentially lethal machinery. But David Bishop evidently hadn't been guilty of that particular error in judgment. He'd owned a cell phone, but it had been in his coat pocket at the time of the accident and unused for any purpose since the previous night. If he'd been distracted, something else was the cause.

I asked some more of the questions I'd put to George Orcutt, with the same lack of results. No, she didn't know David Bishop, couldn't remember ever seeing him prior to the accident. Yes, she knew George Orcutt slightly but couldn't or wouldn't say what she thought of him as a reliable witness.

"Is there anything else you can tell me, Mrs. Blunt? Anything at all that might help clarify what took place that day?"

"I wish there was, but no, I—" She broke off, frowning, the

way you do at a sudden memory jog. "Oh. Oh, wait. Floyd Mears."

"Floyd Mears?"

"I just remembered. He pulled out of the service station in that big white pickup of his just as I passed. Yes, I'm sure he did."

"He was behind you when the accident happened?"

"He must have been. A short distance behind. But he wasn't there when I stopped and got out after the crash."

"Turned off the highway?"

"No, he couldn't have. There's no other road between the service station and Ridgecrest. In all the excitement and confusion I completely forgot about him at the time, or else I'd have told the officers." Mrs. Blunt sat forward, peering at a point over my right shoulder while she worked her memory. "He must have made a sudden U-turn. I seem to have a vague recollection of his pickup going away in the opposite direction."

"So he could also have witnessed the collision."

She said, purse-lipped, "And drove away to avoid becoming involved. That would be just like the man."

I wondered if George Orcutt had seen Floyd Mears following Mrs. Blunt and then U-turn away from the scene of the accident. No surprise that he hadn't told me if so, as uncooperative as he'd been.

"I take it Mears is local," I said. "Do you know him well?"

"No one knows him well. He keeps to himself, hardly has a civil word for anybody."

"Can you tell me where he lives?"

"In the hills somewhere between Rio Verdi and Monte

Rio, I don't know exactly where. Grace Hammond at the market might be able to tell you."

"What does he do for a living?"

"I don't really know, except that he hunts deer and sells venison to Grace now and then. You'd have to ask him."

"I will when I talk to him."

"If you talk to him," Mrs. Blunt said. "He's an unfriendly cuss, Floyd Mears is. I'd be surprised to hear he gave you the time of day, let alone admitted to witnessing the accident."

3

The drizzle had stopped by the time I rolled up and over heavily wooded Walker Hill and picked out the narrow, muddy access lane to Floyd Mears' property from the landmarks Grace Hammond had given me. It was getting on toward four o'clock by then, the combination of overcast sky and dense pine and redwood forest creating a wet, dusklike gloom. If there were any other homes in the vicinity, they were well hidden. It had been a quarter of a mile since the last driveway before this one had appeared and then disappeared among the trees.

I turned in at a crawl in deference to the muddy surface and the fact that the lane led downhill, gradually at first, more steeply and crookedly after I crossed a platform bridge spanning a slender, fast-running creek. I'd gone a hundred yards or so before the lane curved, the trees thinned, and a broad clearing opened up ahead. Not one but three structures squatted there, all of them built of rough-hewn redwood—a good-sized cabin and two outbuildings off to one side.

Floyd Mears was home: a newish, mud-streaked, white four-door Dodge Ram pickup was parked near the largest of the outbuildings and light leaked through the cabin's front window. A little surprisingly, given Earline Blunt's description of him as unfriendly and reclusive, he already had company. A second vehicle, this one a nondescript Ford van several years older, was angled in behind the pickup. The visitor probably reduced even more my chances of getting Mears to talk to me.

I parked and got out onto a rough carpeting of wet pine-needled grass. It was quiet here except for the dripping of rainwater from tree branches and a faint clattering noise that seemed to come from the smallest, shedlike outbuilding. No-body came out of the cabin. That was a little surprising, too. My car is eight years old and not the quietest vehicle on the road; they must have heard me jouncing in along the lane.

There was no front porch, just three steps to a little landing before the door. I went up and used my knuckles—once, twice, three times. Still nobody showed. Well, maybe they were in one of the outbuildings or out in the woods for some reason. Or maybe Mears had seen me through the window and just wasn't opening up to a stranger.

I tried knocking again, gave it up, and slogged over the wet ground toward the other structures. The clattering noise grew louder and I could also hear the throb of a motor as I passed the smaller shed. Generator, a large one with a troublesome bearing—Mears' sole source of electricity, evidently. The only wires anywhere on the property ran from that shed to both its larger neighbor and the cabin.

The other shed was set farther back against the pine woods, its facing side a blank wall against which cordwood was stacked under a hanging tarp. The entrance was around on the near side. When I turned the corner I saw the door—and some-thing else that pulled me up short, set up a prickly sensation on the back of my skull.

A dead dog lay half-hidden in the grass just beyond the door.

Big Doberman, its jaws hinged open and teeth bared in a rictal snarl. A fifteen- or twenty-foot length of chain ran from a leather collar around its neck to an iron spike ring that had been driven into one of the trees. The animal had been there for some time, more than a few hours. Its fur was sodden, there was a buildup of rainwater in its upturned ear pocket, and the two raw wounds that had killed it, one in its side, the other in the ruff of its neck, had been washed free of blood. Bullet wounds. I'd seen enough in my time to identify them without going any closer.

I stood for a couple of seconds, tensed, listening. Rain drip, the hum and clatter of the generator. No other sounds. Then I did an about-face and walked fast back to the car; leaned in to release the catch on the panel beneath the dash where I keep my .38 Colt Bodyguard. Automatic reaction to strange and potentially dangerous surroundings. Better safe than sorry, always.

I slid the weapon into my coat pocket, kept my hand on it as I went back to the shed. Still nothing new to hear on the way, or when I edged up close to the entrance. I banged on the thick, tight-fitting door, using my fist this time. No response. The door was not locked; the knob turned easily when I tried it. All right, then. Illegal trespass is usually a bad idea, but the murdered dog justified it here. I turned the knob all the way, opened the door.

I expected cold semidarkness; what I got was humidity and a blaze of light that made me blink and squint. Both light and humidity came from a series of high-wattage LED hooded reflectors hanging in rows over three-quarters of the interior. Beneath them, on shelves, were dozens of green plants in various stages of growth. The shed had no windows, but ducting ran from an exhaust fan into a hole cut in the back wall. There was a small dehumidifier, and gardening tools, paper bags, and a loose scattering of plastic containers on a workbench. The containers were empty except for a greenish-gray residue. More of the same substance, a mixture of dried, shredded leaves, stems, seeds, and flower buds, was sprinkled over the bench top.

Indoor pot farm.

So now I knew what Floyd Mears did for a living. Not that I cared much in principle; marijuana growing and selling is already legal in some states and others would soon follow, California included. Everybody to his vice, as long as no innocent parties get hurt in the process. Except that innocent parties do get hurt sometimes, and not only humans. That Doberman outside. Guard dog, probably. Blown away by somebody who wanted access to cured weed ready for smoking and/or sale. The containers strewn over the bench, another that had fallen to the floor, indicated a quick search and grab.

A bad feeling had begun to work in me. There was no sign of either Mears or his visitor in here. The cabin, then? I backed out of the shed, shut the door, crossed back over there.

The first thing I did was stretch up on the spongy ground under the window and look through a narrow aperture between the curtain halves. All I could see was a small section of the front room. Table, one chair toppled on its side, and another upright at a skewed angle as if it had been violently shoved backward. The only other things I could make out were a woodstove and a small stack of cordwood.

I did not want to go inside. But the bad feeling was even stronger now, and there are some things you simply can't avoid doing. If the cabin was empty, then all right, I could drive away from here without any further involvement and with a clear conscience. The murder of the dog and running of a small-scale marijuana farm were misdemeanors and none of my business as such.

If the cabin was empty.

But it wasn't.

The door was unlocked, so access was no problem. I rapped on it again, waited, then shoved it open wide and leaned in without entering. I could see more of the room then. Part of a larder and a makeshift kitchen with a kerosene stove, an open doorway into what was probably a bedroom—and a dead man sprawled across the threshold.

He lay twisted on his right side, his face turned toward me. A welter of dried blood shone darkly across the fronts of an open leather jacket and white shirt. Shot like the Doberman. How many times I couldn't tell. Not self-inflicted, even though there was a gun, what looked to be a Saturday night special, loosely clenched in one outflung hand.

That should have been enough for me to keep from entering, but it wasn't. One man dead, two vehicles parked in the yard—that didn't add up the way it should. I went on in.

Murder, all right.

Two victims, not just one.

The second dead man was in a seated posture on the floor, propped against the wall on the far side of the room, his legs spread out in an inverted V. Blood all over him, too, and streaked down the rough-hewn boards above him. Shot while backing up and the force of impact had slammed him into the wall. On the planking beside the body was a large-caliber automatic on an aluminum frame. I couldn't tell how many times he had been hit, either, but it was plain enough that they'd both cut loose with several rounds each; bullet holes pocked the walls at both ends of the room.

I'm no stranger to crime scenes, God knows, but a double homicide like this was something new and ugly in my experience. And the way I'd walked into it gave it an even more nightmarish quality. Drive up to the Russian River on a routine job, get a name I'd never heard before as a possible accident witness, come out here and stumble onto a shed full of marijuana and a dog and two strangers shot to death. One of those crazy zigzags that leave you feeling unlucky and faintly disoriented.

I stood motionless for several seconds, sucking deep lungfuls of cold air, automatically taking in details. The corpse on the floor between the two rooms: forty or so, short red hair, fireplug build, dressed in the once-white shirt and corduroy jacket and a pair of slacks. The one sitting against the wall: a few years older, thickset, beard-stubbled jowls, bald except for thin comb-over strands of straggly brown hair, wearing Levi's and a plaid lumberman's shirt. Mears? The room was cold and damp—no fire in the woodstove in a long while; the all too familiar stench of sudden violent death was faint, and from the appearance of the bodies, rigor had come and gone. The shootings must have taken place sometime last night.

Marijuana deal gone bad, the way it looked—the kind of thing that happens all too often these days, though it usually involves large and street-valuable amounts of weed. Both men armed, an argument of some kind, out came the guns like a couple of trigger-happy cowboys drawing on each other in a western B movie, and they'd blazed away until they were both down for the count. That kind of stupid scenario.

A little funny that such a thing would happen here, considering the kind of small growing operation I'd seen in the shed. Not that it mattered as far as I was concerned. The local law's headache, not mine.

I backed out of there, opened my cell phone on the way to the car. The fact that I was able to get a clear signal in a place surrounded by dense forest was a relief.

4

Crime scene investigation, whether big city, suburban, or rural, pretty much follows the same established pattern. Slow, methodical, meticulous routine. I'd been through it so many times, as investigating officer and witness both, I could write a full-length, dully repetitive book about my experiences. When you're in the position I was in here, it's a tedious and seemingly interminable process made even worse by the fact that I was dealing with strangers in unfamiliar, somewhat isolated territory.

The routine is unpleasant no matter which side you're on, but easier if you're part of the crew because you're busy all the while. For a material witness it's static and numbing. Sit and wait, answer questions from the first responders, sit and wait, answer questions from the second wave and men in charge, sit and wait some more. The only good part was that no suspicion was directed at me once I showed my ID and explained the job that had brought me to Rio Verdi and then to Floyd Mears' property. For most of the three-plus hours I was required to remain on the scene I was shunted out of the way and left alone.

Cell phone reception was pretty good here; I called Tamara, who was still at the agency, to tell her what had gone down today, then Kerry at Bates and Carpenter and Emily at home to let them know I'd be late and not to wait dinner. All I said to them was that I'd gotten unavoidably hung up; they did not need to know the unpleasant details. After that I sat in the car and vegetated. Jake Runyon has a knack for shutting himself down at times like this, sort of like a computer put into sleep mode, but I've never been able to master that ability. My thoughts tend to run riot while I'm on a protracted wait, skipping from one subject to another indiscriminately, so that I end up feeling antsy and disgruntled. Patience has never been one of my long suits even at the best of times.

The officer in charge, a county sheriff's department lieutenant named Heidegger, came around and finally told me I was free to leave. He'd been brusquely efficient in his questioning earlier, but now he just seemed solemn and tired. He was about fifty, thick bodied, square shouldered—a career law officer who'd evidently dealt with as much if not more violence than I had and almost but not quite become inured to it.

"Regular shooting gallery in there," he said. "We counted nine rounds fired, four hits and five misses."

"Gunslingers," I said.

"Yeah. One of the dead guys is Floyd Mears. I guess you figured that. The other, according to the wallet we found on him, is Ray Fentress, *F-e-n-t-r-e-s-s,* address in your city. Name mean anything to you?"

"Ray Fentress. No."

"And you'd never seen him before?"

"Never saw either of them before."

"Reason I asked is that I called in for a computer check on the name and he's an ex-con, less than a week out of Mule Creek after doing eighteen months on an assault conviction." Mule Creek was a minimum-security prison in Ione, up in the foothills east of Sacramento. "What I can't figure is why he'd come all the way up here to buy dope from a small-timer like Mears."

"Some past tie between them, maybe."

"Sure, but why come armed? Why deal with a man, even one you knew personally, if you thought you needed self-protection?"

"Self-protection might not be the reason."

"Robbery?"

"Could be, if there was a lot of cannabis and money at stake."

"But there wasn't," Heidegger said. "Not that we've been able to find. Just a small amount of weed in one of Fentress' pockets, couldn't be worth more than a few hundred dollars at street prices, and a stash in Mears' bedroom worth about the same. And less than seventy-five dollars cash total on the two of them, their vehicles, and the premises."

"Well, the get-together last night could've been to set up a deal for later, and for some reason it went prematurely sour."

"That's a possibility."

"I can think of another explanation," I said. "Third party involved. Somebody who shot both men and then the dog for however much dope was stored in the shed."

"Yeah, that occurred to me, too," Heidegger said. "But there doesn't seem to be much doubt that Mears and Fentress blew each other away, and unless we find out Mears' cottage industry was a lot bigger than what's in that shed, there wouldn't have been enough weed or cash to make anybody in his right mind commit homicide."

"Then who shot the Doberman? And why? And when?"

"Fentress, so he could get into the shed to get the dope we found on him. Mears came home and caught him, Fentress threw down on him, they went into the cabin to talk things over—"

"—and Mears pulled his piece and the shooting started. Makes sense, I guess."

"As much as any other explanation," Heidegger said. "I'll tell you, I hate complicated crimes. I sure hope this one turns out to be just what it looks like." He sighed heavily. "None of your worry in any case. I'll need a written statement from you, but we can do that by fax. Unless your accident investigation brings you back up to the county in the near future."

"Doesn't look as though it will, now."

And finally I was out of there for the long drive home.

I faxed my statement to the Sonoma County sheriff's department the following day, and that should have been the end of my involvement. But it wasn't. The world is a sometimes strange and perverse place, as we all know from experience, and my profession occasionally fraught with the kind of unforeseen twists that had led me to Floyd Mears in the first place.

It was nearly three days before I found this out. Little enough happened during those sixty-some hours. I wrote and delivered the deposition, then wrote and delivered my report to our client, the attorney representing Arthur Clements, in which I provided a brief explanation of how I'd learned of the now-dead third witness to the Rio Verdi accident and what had transpired afterward. All that remained of that case would be delivery of subpoenas to George Orcutt and Earline Blunt once the trial date was set, should the attorney decide to utilize us for the task. Probably not, though; independent process servers come cheaper than a small but upscale private agency.

There were no new developments in the double homicide. Tamara followed the news stories on the Internet and gave me capsule summaries; I have a long-standing aversion to daily doses of current events in the media, crime news in particular, and so actively avoid reading both newspapers and online news sites. There was additional proof, though not conclusive proof, that Floyd Mears and Ray Fentress had shot each other during an argument over money or marijuana or both: the Saturday night special in Fentress' hand had done for both Mears and the Doberman, the .45 by Mears' body had taken out Fentress, and nitrate tests confirmed that both men had discharged firearms. Lieutenant Heidegger hadn't yet ruled out the possibility of a third party as either shooter or thief; however, the investigation was ongoing.

As for criminal records, Mears had none of any kind and the assault conviction that had landed Fentress in Mule Creek for eighteen months was his only offense and had nothing to do with drugs. He'd been spotted speeding on Mission Street not far from his Excelsior District home, for some reason tried to outrun the police cruiser and sideswiped two parked cars, and then stupidly resisted arrest by assaulting one of the officers and breaking his arm in the ensuing struggle. Fentress' blood alcohol level was 0.28, well over the legal limit. As a first-time offender he might have been given a lighter or even a suspended sentence at his trial, but he'd had the misfortune to draw an inexperienced public defender and a hard-nosed judge. Fentress' refusal to provide a satisfactory explanation for his panicked behavior also mitigated against leniency.

How Fentress and Mears had come in contact was a mystery. Nothing had turned up to indicate they'd known each other prior to that night, or linking them in any other way. Fentress' wife had no idea and in fact vehemently denied that her husband was in any way involved with marijuana. Based on his photograph, nobody in the Russian River area owned up to having seen him before. A couple of Rio Verdi residents admitted to having heard rumors that Mears grew and sold pot to a carefully selected group of local customers. Who those customers were they couldn't or wouldn't say.

All pretty standard stuff, at least on the surface. Ex-con is released from prison, gets a dealer's name somewhere, goes off to make a buy, there's trouble over price or amount, and both men end up dead. Still, there were a lot of unanswered questions. The ones Heidegger and I had discussed. And others: Why would Fentress have driven all the way up to the Russian River to make a buy, even if he knew Mears, when you can score pot on just about any street corner in San Francisco? Why had he taken a gun with him? Protection? To rip off Mears? Neither of those answers seemed likely: small-time dealer, relatively small amounts of weed, no large amount of cash on the premises, and Fentress had no record of violent crime other than his drunken assault on the cop. Before that Fentress had worked for a Millbrae-based landscaping firm—from all indications, just another average law-abiding citizen.

The media played up the mystery angle a bit, especially in Sonoma County, but there wasn't enough juice for the story to have legs. It was already beginning to fade under the weight of more sensational news by the morning of the third day. Fading in my mind, too, by force of will as much as anything else. Too many crime scenes, too much blood and gore for me to dwell on it as it was.

I was home that third day, a Friday. One of my nonworking, free to enjoy my semiretirement days. Right. What I was doing when Tamara called was replacing a defective P trap on the kitchen sink. Down on the floor on my already-aching back, wrench in hand and face speckled with scummy drip as I dismantled the old trap and replaced it, Shameless the cat rubbing around me and purring as if he thought I was playing a game for his amusement. I had just finished tightening the upper ring seal on the new trap when my cell phone went off. I would not have answered it if the thing hadn't been in my shirt pocket and I wasn't ready for a break to ease the stiffness in my back.

"Sorry to bother you," Tamara said, "but I figured you'd want to know."

"Know what?"

"You busy? You sound busy."

"I was, but I'm almost done. Know what?"

"A woman came in a few minutes ago asking for you. I told her it was your day off and you'd be in the office on Monday, but she doesn't want to wait that long. Practically begged me to call you. She's waiting out in the anteroom now."

"What does she want?"

"She wouldn't tell me. Has to be you."

"Why? Who is she?"

"Doreen Fentress. Ray Fentress' widow."

5

Doreen Fentress was one of the saddest-looking women I'd ever seen. It was not just the obvious grief she was suffering; it was a deeply ingrained melancholy, a defining part of her like something in her DNA. She was a too-thin dishwater blonde about the same age as her late husband, or maybe a few years older. It was difficult to be sure because of the lines in a narrow face that gave the impression of drooping, as if it were pale-colored wax instead of flesh that formed her features. One long look at her and another into liquidy brown eyes like those of an abandoned puppy and I was pretty sure of two things: I was not going to like what she wanted of me, yet I might be disposed to accommodate her anyway if I could.

She didn't seem to mind the fact that it had taken me more than an hour to get cleaned up and drive down to South Park from Diamond Heights. She hadn't had an easy life, that was plain, but one thing it had taught her was something I lacked: patience. All she said when I walked into the agency and Tamara came out and introduced us was, "Thank you for seeing me. I wouldn't have asked if it wasn't important." Diffident and deferential, too. Oh, yeah, she had me hooked already.

We went into my office. She walked stiffly, as if her feet or maybe her back hurt. The connecting door to Tamara's office was closed, but my partner is an inquisitive and sometimes rash young woman; I would not be surprised to find out later that she had an eavesdropping ear to the panel on her side.

I said, "I'm sorry for your loss, Mrs. Fentress," when she and I were seated. The words had a hollow, awkward ring, as they always do when you say them to a stranger.

"Thank you. It was . . . a terrible shock. Ray was only home a week. Seven days, that was all we had after eighteen months apart. You know he was in prison?"

"Yes."

"For a foolish crime he committed while he was drunk, God knows why. There's no doubt he was guilty of that. But what happened up north, what they claim he did there . . . no. No."

I didn't say anything. Family members often staunchly believe their husbands, wives, sons, daughters, are innocent, no matter how serious the crimes or how much evidence there might be to the contrary.

"He didn't do it," she said again. "He didn't kill that man Mears. Or shoot that poor dog, either. He loved dogs . . . we have one of our own."

"The crime scene evidence says otherwise."

Vehement headshake: disbelief, denial. "It's wrong, that's all; it couldn't have happened the way it looked. Ray never owned a handgun. A hunting rifle, yes, he used to go deer hunting sometimes, but not a handgun. He wouldn't have one in the house."

Maybe that was because he'd never had need of one before. I could have said as much. I could also have told her how easily almost anybody, and particularly a man who'd just been released from prison, could buy a Saturday night special on the streets on short notice. Or reminded her of the fact that the forensic tests proved he'd fired the one found in his hand. But none of that would have swayed her, so I said nothing at all.

She said, "Whatever Ray's reason for going to see Floyd Mears, he didn't bring a gun with him and it couldn't have had anything to do with marijuana. Please believe me."

I said carefully, "Mrs. Fentress, it makes no difference whether I believe you or not. It's strictly a police matter—"

"He had asthma," she said.

". . . How's that again?"

"Ray. He had severe asthma. He didn't smoke; he couldn't stand to be in a room with anyone who did."

"Well . . . some asthmatics claim that marijuana doesn't affect—"

"Ray wasn't one of them."

"You do know the investigating officers found a Baggie of it in his coat pocket? Three hundred dollars' worth."

"Somebody put it there, the same person who put the gun in his hand." When I made no comment, she said, "You think he might have picked up the habit in prison," which was exactly what I was thinking. Cons in lockups like Mule Creek have more ways than you might think of obtaining drugs. "But you're wrong. He never smoked a joint in his life—he *couldn't*, I tell you. His asthma was so bad he had to carry an extrapowerful prescription inhaler to prevent severe attacks. That's one of the reasons, the main one, we were planning to move."

"Move?"

"To Arizona or New Mexico, we hadn't decided which.

Someplace where the air is dry. Someplace where nobody knew he'd been in prison."

"When were you planning to leave?"

"At the end of the next week. I've already given notice at the store in Stonestown where I work." Her mouth bent downward at the corners, making the facial droop seem even more pronounced. "Now . . . If they don't hire me back I don't know what I'll do."

"How were you going to finance the move?"

"Finance it? Oh . . . I managed to save some money while Ray was . . . away. Not a lot, but enough for a new start. And Ray said he might be able to get a loan to help us out."

"Oh? From whom?"

"A friend. Joe Buckner."

"How large a loan?"

"He didn't say, but it couldn't have been very much. Joe isn't well-off; he works as a bartender."

"Did Buckner agree to the loan?"

"I don't know if Ray had asked him yet."

I let a few seconds slide away before I said, "Do you know if your husband was acquainted with Floyd Mears?"

"He never mentioned the name to me. Or said anything about the Russian River—it's not a place we ever went to."

"Yet he went to see Mears that night."

"I can't imagine why. I wish to God I knew."

"Where did he tell you he was going?"

"He didn't. All he said was that he had some business to attend to and he might be back late."

"How did he seem when he left?"

"Seem?"

"His mood, his frame of mind."

She chewed at her underlip. "A little . . . I don't know, a little nervous. But he was that way from the time he came home."

"I have to say this, Mrs. Fentress. It's possible your husband had no intention of asking his friend Buckner for a loan. There's another way he could have gotten money to help finance your move, another explanation for why he went to see Mears."

"What do you mean?"

"Marijuana is a highly salable commodity, as I'm sure you know."

"You think Ray— No. He wasn't a thief and he would never have sold drugs." She drew a deep, shuddery breath. "My husband made mistakes, God knows, but he was a good man at heart. I was married to him for nineteen years. Don't you think I would have known if he wasn't?"

Not necessarily. Nobody knows anybody all that well, spouses included. Spouses especially in some cases. I thought that, and then I thought cynically: Salt of the earth, Ray Fentress. Incapable of killing, except where four-footed animals like deer were concerned; never owned a handgun, never smoked, and wouldn't ever sell dope. Good husband, good man at heart, hardworking average citizen. Until he drove drunk one night, resisted arrest and assaulted a police officer, and got himself locked up in a cell for eighteen months.

I said, "Why did you want to see me, Mrs. Fentress? I can't tell you anything to ease your mind, and if you're thinking of hiring me to investigate the shootings, I couldn't oblige you if I wanted to. A private detective has no legal right to interfere in an open homicide case."

"It's not open, it's closed. The man in charge up there, I can't remember his name—"

"Lieutenant Heidegger."

"Yes. He as much as told me so."

I doubted that. No homicide investigation, especially one with as many quirks and questions as this one, gets marked closed in only three days. Still, inasmuch as Heidegger and his crew hadn't turned up any new evidence and the sheriff's department likely was overworked and understaffed, they might well be leaning toward an acceptance of the most obvious explanation. The lieutenant wouldn't have told Doreen Fentress that, but then he might have said something to her that hinted at it.

"I'm sorry," I said, "truly, but that's not official and probably won't be for some time. I could have my license suspended if I tried to mount an investigation of my own."

"Couldn't you do something else for me?" The liquidy brown eyes added mute appeal to her words.

"Such as?"

"Try to prove I'm right about the kind of man my husband was. Try to find out how he knew Floyd Mears, why he went to see him that night. That's not the same thing as investigating the murders, is it?"

"Well, technically, no, but—"

"I'll pay you whatever you ask until all the money I have runs out."

"It's not a matter of money, Mrs. Fentress. Or rather it is where you're concerned. What you're asking would likely be a fruitless undertaking and you'd be depleting your savings for nothing."

"I don't care about my savings. You're a detective, a good one according to what I've read; you have ways of finding things out. You could try, couldn't you?" When I didn't answer, she said with desperation rising in her voice, "I can't stand living the rest of my life not knowing. Even if it turns out I'm wrong and Ray did intend to rob Mears, even if he was a . . . a killer after all, I'd rather know than not know. You understand?"

All too well. I nodded.

"Then please help me. Please try to find out."

Thankless job, nowhere job. Waste of her money, waste of my time. I'd have to notify Heidegger, get his permission for an offshoot investigation. I'd have to go poking into a dead ex-con's life before and after his prison sentence with little enough hope of finding out something that would relieve Doreen Fentress' burden of grief. I'd be a damn fool to make the effort. I'd be a damn fool to say yes, okay, I'll see what I can do.

"Yes, okay," I said, "I'll see what I can do."

6

Tamara didn't think much of my decision, either. She'd been listening at the door, all right, and when Doreen Fentress was gone she came out of her office and admitted it. When I suggested that she could have waited to hear the gist of the conversation from me, she said, "Well, I was curious after the silent treatment she gave me. No secrets around here, right?"

"Not when it comes to business, anyway."

"What's that mean?"

Whoops. Indirect reference to her recent disinclination to discuss her love life, which she'd always done before with casual candor and in more detail than I cared to know. But since she'd taken up again with her musician boyfriend, Horace Fields, after his return to the city following a failed near marriage, she hardly even mentioned his name. Maybe it was because she knew I had my doubts about the wisdom of hooking up with him again after the shabby way he'd treated her the first time around, but more likely it was because things weren't going well between them. There'd been little indications that led me to suspect this was the case—grumpy mornings, puffy eyes indicating lack of sleep, long, brooding silences.

But I hadn't made any attempt to pry; it would only have created unnecessary friction between us. Even an oblique reference was a mistake on a day when she was in a more or less upbeat mood. None of my business anyway unless she brought up the subject or her relationship with Horace affected her work, which so far it hadn't.

"Doesn't mean anything," I said. "Just something irrelevant you say without thinking."

"Sort of like a mouth fart."

I had to grin at that. "Sort of."

"Well, anyhow, it's a good thing you didn't make the Fentress woman any promises. Fifty-fifty the Sonoma sheriff's department says stay out of it."

"More like seventy-five twenty-five they'll allow it. Lieutenant Heidegger didn't strike me as a hardnose and I can promise him I won't step on any official toes."

She gave me one of her Tamara the No-Nonsense Businesswoman looks. "You wouldn't be thinking of a pro bono investigation, would you? Assuming you get the go-ahead."

"No. We'll charge Mrs. Fentress expenses and a nominal fee if nothing comes of it. Full agency rates if I turn up answers for her."

"Which you probably won't."

"Which I probably won't, but I'll give it my best shot."

"You always do."

"Correction: we always do. I'm going to need some Internet help from you."

"Uh-huh. Tamara the techno slave," she said, and pooched up her face and rolled her eyes in that way she had. Whenever she did it, I was oddly reminded of Hattie McDaniel in the actress' pre–*Gone with the Wind* days. As round and plump and dark as Tamara was, she even looked a little like Hattie McDaniel when she did the face-pooching, eye-rolling thing. Not that I'd ever said as much to her. If I had, she would probably and with some justification have accused me of racial stereotyping and brained me with her computer keyboard.

I put in a call to Lieutenant Heidegger in Santa Rosa, or tried to; he wasn't available. I left my name and both office and cell numbers and asked for a callback at his earliest convenience. It being Friday afternoon, I didn't expect to hear from him until Monday, but he surprised me. The return call came in less than half an hour. I was still at my desk; going straight home would have meant finishing up the plumbing job and dealing with more household chores. So I'd decided to stick around and do some paperwork on an employee background check for one of the new dot-com companies that had infested the city—*infested* being an apt term because the proliferation had driven real estate prices to exorbitant levels and caused a lot of small businesses and private residents to sell out and move elsewhere.

Heidegger had no objections to what Mrs. Fentress wanted me to do. He'd have to check with his superiors, he said, but as far as he was concerned I could go ahead as long as I stayed within the established boundaries and immediately turned over to him anything pertinent I might happen to find out. Then he said, "Frankly, I think it's a waste of time. Pretty clear-cut that Fentress went to see Mears to buy or steal weed and the two of them ended up blowing each other away. I just don't see any other explanation."

"So the case will probably end in the closed file."

"Looks that way. You sure you want to work for the widow? She's bound to wind up disappointed."

"I know it. But she practically begged me and I never could say no to a bereaved party."

"Well, it's your time and her money. Good luck."

"Thanks. I'll need it."

I went into Tamara's office, waited until she finished what she was working on and looked up from her Mac before I spoke. "Looks like it's a go. Can you squeeze in a few searches for me?"

"Grumbling all the while," she said, and softened the words with one of her quirky smiles. "Fentress, Mears. Who else?"

"Fentress' friends and former employer. Short list of three."

"Names?"

"What, you mean you didn't write them down while you were eavesdropping?"

"Ha-ha."

"Joseph Buckner, bartender at the Bighorn Tavern in the Excelsior," I said after consulting my notes. "Peter Retzyck, *R-e-t-z-y-c-k*, works in a sporting goods store in the same neighborhood. As far as Mrs. Fentress knows, those are the only two her husband had any contact with since he got out of Mule Creek. The former employer is Philip Kennedy, owner of Kennedy Landscape Designs in Millbrae. Fentress had been on the job there seven years when he was arrested on the assault charge."

Tamara finished typing the names into a new file. "Okay. That all for now?"

"Unless you turn up some other names."

She didn't. Her preliminary searches revealed no new names worth consulting and no new information that pertained to Fentress. Mears had no criminal record, the only official blot being a domestic violence incident with a woman in Monte

Rio who refused to press charges. Buckner and Kennedy were solid citizens, at least insofar as the law was concerned. Retzyck had one D&D and one arrest for the illegal purchase of an assault weapon that had gotten him a slap-on-the-wrist fine, both more than four years ago.

So the leads I had to work with were pretty slim, as expected. I'd closed cases starting with fewer and slimmer before; maybe I'd get lucky with this one, even though the odds were stacked against it. And maybe if I did get lucky, it would be in a way that gave Doreen Fentress some closure and peace of mind. Depressing as hell, the prospect of having to face her one final time with dead-end news.

Well, I'd have no one to blame but myself if that was how it turned out. Me and my ever-bleeding heart.

I dislike and begrudge conducting agency business on week-ends. Saturdays and Sundays are reserved for time with Kerry and Emily—picnics, museum and aquarium visits in Golden Gate Park, baseball games in season, drives in the country, lunches and dinners at old-favorite restaurants. So optimally I would have spent this Saturday in the bosom of my family and started in on the Fentress matter on Monday. But circum-stances conspired to change the game plan.

Emily had made a bowling date with some of her friends and didn't want to break it. The friends included a couple of males, a fact she readily admitted, but that was all right. My adopted daughter is as trustworthy as any almost-fifteen-year-old can be, and brighter and more grounded than at least 95 percent of her peers. Proud papa, sure, that's me, but one with justification and without blinders; she truly is an exceptional young lady. And I'd learned to accept the fact, somewhat grudgingly, that teenagers as they grow older neither want nor need to spend as much of their free time in the company of Mom and Pop as they had in their younger days.

Kerry was busy, too. One way in which she was coping with her mother's death in late November was the assembling of a three-volume collection of Cybil's pulp magazine stories about hard-boiled detective Samuel Leatherman. Together we'd found a small e-book and print on demand publisher who agreed to bring out all three volumes, as well as to reprint Cybil's two retro Leatherman novels, *Dead Eye* and *Black Eye*. Kerry was in the process of writing lengthy introductions to each of the five editions—a highly therapeutic undertaking that I had no intention of interrupting. Her health was good now, no recurrence of the breast cancer and no more lingering physical or emotional effects of the abduction ordeal she'd suffered last summer, but Cybil's death had been another harsh blow to her still-fragile psyche. The loss would have been even more devastating without the creation of what amounted to a shrine to her mother's memory.

So I was at loose ends this day, and the prospect of sitting around the condo by myself held little appeal. And it so happened that Joe Buckner worked the day shift weekends at the Bighorn Tavern—Tamara was nothing if not thorough in her searches. Why not drive over to the Excelsior District, then, and conduct the interview with him today? It shouldn't take long and it would be one less task I'd have to face next week. Two, maybe, if it turned out that Pete Retzyck worked Saturdays at Mission Sporting Goods.

7

The Excelsior District runs along Mission Street east of San Jose Avenue and south of Highway 280, on the way into Daly City. I'd known the neighborhood well at one time, the Outer Mission being where I was born and raised, but it had changed quite a bit since I was a kid. Once mainly an Italian and Irish enclave, it was now a polyglot of ethnic groups—Chinese, Mexican, Central American, and Filipino predominating— and working-class Caucasians, most of whom had been long-time residents. It has been described as a kind of urban Main Street, U.S.A., with restaurants, coffee shops, markets, baker-ies, boutiques, hair salons, and hardware stores all within a range of several blocks, but then you could say the same about other San Francisco neighborhoods. For me it had become less and less familiar over the years. Whenever I went there, I couldn't help feeling pangs of nostalgia for what it used to be—for the old days even though they hadn't all been good old days growing up.

The Bighorn Tavern, to my surprise, was a relic of those old days. Tucked between an Asian market and a dry-cleaning business, it had an old-fashioned, neon-free façade, its only

advertisement being its name imprinted on the opaque window next to the entrance door. Ray Fentress had probably been
drawn to it because it was located within a couple of blocks of
where he'd lived with his wife on Lisbon Street, and because
it would cater to his type of nonethnic clientele—a blue-collar
white man's comfort zone.

The interior bore out my external assessment. Weakly lit,
musty with the smells of beer, alcohol, ingrained traces of to-
bacco smoke from the days before the no-smoking laws were
passed. As you'd expect from its name, the walls were decorated
with deer heads and racks of antlers, all very old and dusty looking; otherwise there was nothing to distinguish it from dozens
of similar watering holes in the city, thousands of others spread
across the country. The foot-railed bar extended the length of
the right-hand wall; a line of high-backed wooden booths ran
along the wall opposite. Two pool tables and two pinball machines were stuffed into an alcove at the rear.

The Bighorn had been in business for a lot of years, obviously. It might even have been in operation when I was growing up not far away with my alcoholic father and long-suffering
mother. Hell, the old man might even have hoisted a few here
himself on one of his all too frequent pub crawls.

There weren't many customers now, at a few minutes past
one o'clock. The booths were all empty and only four people,
three men and a woman, occupied the cracked leatherette
stools at the bar. The men, all middle-aged and dressed in work
clothes, were drinking beer; the woman, a blowsy blonde whose
age could have been anywhere between forty and sixty, was
sipping on something that, judging from the shape of the glass
and the pale color of its contents, was either a gin or vodka
martini. She gave me a blearily hopeful look as I slid onto a

stool as far from her and the men as I could get, but when I didn't return her smile she wiped it off and put her attention back on her drink.

The man behind the plank looked to be in his mid-forties, thick through the chest and shoulders, lantern jaw, a tonsure of light-colored hair around the back of his skull and a lone patch in front like a tiny island in a dry lake bed. He looked me over long enough to determine I was a stranger, but he seemed welcoming enough when he said, "Afternoon. What'll it be?"

"Anchor Steam, draft if you have it. And some conversation."

"The beer I got."

He moved down the bar to fill a glass. When he brought it back and set it down, I said in a lowered voice, "Are you Joe Buckner?"

"That's right. Why?"

"I'd like to talk to you about Ray Fentress."

That put him on his guard. "Why?" he said again.

"You know what happened to him?"

"Yeah, I heard. Who're you?"

I said, "The man who found him and Floyd Mears," and added my name and a reminder of my profession.

"I don't believe it," Buckner said.

"You don't believe what? That I'm who I say I am?"

He leaned forward. "No, that Ray shot it out with some backwoods marijuana dealer. That's bullshit, plain and simple."

"Not according to the evidence."

"Yeah, well, whatever. But the Ray I knew was no killer. And no damn pothead. He had bad asthma, he couldn't stand smoke."

"So his wife told me."

"Doreen? How do you know her?"

"She doesn't believe the evidence, either—she thinks he had some other reason for going to see Mears. She came to my office yesterday, begged me to try to prove her right. She told me you were a good friend of her husband's; that's why I'm here."

"Good enough not to blow him off like most of his other so-called friends when he got sent to prison. The only one besides me who'd have anything to do with him when he came home was Pete Retzyck. Doreen give you his name, too?"

"Yes. You know Retzyck, I take it."

"Sure I know him. He's a regular here like Ray was. Two of them used to go hunting together."

"Do you happen to know if he works Saturdays?"

"I don't think so. But I can tell you where he lives. He—"

The blowsy blonde rattled her glass on the bar and called out in a wheedling tone, "Hey, Joe, I'm dry here, Joe."

Buckner said to me, "Just a minute," and went down to the blonde. "No more, Angie, I told you that before. You're over the tab limit."

"One more, huh? Just one?"

"No."

"C'mon, sweetie, be nice. Just a little one?"

"Go home, Angie."

"I'm good for it, you know that; I always pay my tab."

"Yeah, sure you do. A few bucks a month, like interest on a credit card."

She looked my way, looked at the beer drinkers. "Would one of you gentlemen be so kind as to buy a lady one little drink?"

None of us answered her. I knew her type well enough— alone, lonely, desperate for companionship, and looking for solace in the bottom of an empty glass when it wasn't forthcoming—and I felt a little sorry for her. But not enough to act as an enabler for her alcoholism.

Buckner said, "You going to walk out under your own power, or you want me to carry you?"

"Well, all right, you don't have to get tough about it." She lifted herself off the stool with the aid of the beveled edge of the bar. "I'm never coming back here again. Pay my tab with a check. You'll never see me again."

"Promises, promises," one of the beer drinkers said. For some reason the other two thought this was funny. The blonde glared at them, straightened her skirt, and went out with a slow, walk-a-straight-line kind of dignity.

Buckner came back to me. "Drunks," he said. Then he said, "I'll tell you something about Doreen. Woman's a saint. Ray, well, he was no world-beater, but she stood by him through the rough patches, waited for him while he was in Mule Creek. Visited him whenever she could; I drove her up there a couple of times myself. Loyal, you know?"

"Uh-huh."

"So you do a good job for her, man; don't try to take advantage."

"I won't. You don't have to worry about that."

He nodded his head, then flicked it sideways. "That's another thing I can't figure," he said. "Ray doing what he did that got him put in prison. Driving drunk, resisting arrest, assaulting a cop. Just not like him at all."

"No?"

"Hell, no. He wasn't a heavy boozer, didn't usually drink more than a few beers. I only seen him drunk a couple of times in the ten years I knew him. Not aggressive, neither. No fights, no trouble. Easygoing."

"Why was he drinking heavily that night?"

"He never told nobody. But he wasn't his old self for a month or so before it happened, all wound up about something and hitting the sauce kind of hard—I figure it must've been money worries. You know, bills piling up and all that."

"One of those rough patches you mentioned."

"Yeah. Him and Doreen, they were doing all right until she had some female problems a few years ago that cost a bundle. They didn't have no health insurance."

Like too many others in this best of all countries. "How often did you see Ray after he got out?"

Buckner hesitated before he said, "Twice. We had a meal together a couple of days after."

"Did he say anything at all about the Russian River?"

"No."

"Ask you for a loan?"

"A loan? No. Why should he?"

"He told his wife he was going to."

"Yeah? That doesn't make sense. I don't have an extra pot to piss in and he knew it. What would he want a loan for?"

"To help finance a move to Arizona or New Mexico. You knew about that?"

"Sure, Ray told me. He was stoked about it, making a new start somewhere that was better for his asthma, buying an orchard farm. That was always his big dream."

"Buying a farm? How would he pay for it?"

"Money Doreen saved while he was away. She worked two jobs after he went to jail. Worked like a dog."

I didn't doubt that. But her two jobs were department store clerk and part-time housecleaner, neither of which paid well enough to cover monthly bills and leave enough left over to build the kind of stake it takes for a property purchase. The impression I'd had from her was that the amount of her savings was modest at best. And their chances of getting a bank loan, with his record, were slim and none. Ray Fentress might just have been blowing smoke. Either that, or he expected to make a substantial score on his own. By robbing a small-time pot dealer at gunpoint?

While I was ruminating, one of the beer drinkers called for a refill. Buckner went to accommodate him, and when he returned he said, "Listen, I probably shouldn't tell you this, but I guess you oughta know as long as you don't say anything to Doreen about it. She's had enough grief as it is."

"That bad, whatever it is?"

"No. It's just . . . ah, hell, I don't know if it means anything or not. Just keep it to yourself, all right?"

"If I can. I'm obligated to inform a client of anything directly related to my investigation."

"I don't see how this could be related."

"Then it'll just be between you and me."

"Okay, then. Second time I saw Ray was in here two days before he was killed, with a woman I never seen before."

"You know who she was?"

"Mary something, that's all. Thing was, Ray didn't expect me to be here."

"Oh?"

"Late afternoon and I was working nights that week. I come in early, like I do sometimes, and the two of them was in one of the booths over there, drinking beer with their heads together. Ray jumped a little when he saw me, had this kind of guilty look on his face. You know, like a kid caught with his hand in the cookie jar."

"You think she might've been a working girl?"

"I didn't get that hit off her," Buckner said. "Hell, this is the last place he'd have met up with her if she was. Besides, Ray, he wasn't the type to traffic with whores."

"How about other kinds of women?"

"You mean was he a chaser?" Buckner barked a scornful laugh. "Not Ray, uh-uh. As faithful to Doreen as she was to him, swear it on a Bible."

Faithful before he got sent up, okay, but prison changes a man. In some cases gives him appetites he didn't have before. But I kept the thought to myself. "What do you suppose their relationship was?"

"Beats me. I asked him, 'Who's your friend?' and he said, 'Mary,' kind of blurted it out. She didn't say anything, just glared at him as if she didn't like him saying even half her name. They left right after that. I asked Larry, the day barman, how long they'd been there and he told me about fifteen minutes. They didn't come in together—her first, then Ray."

"What did she look like?"

"Around thirty-five. Blond hair, the dye job kind. Not bad looking if you like the hard type. Nice figure"—Buckner lifted his hands ten inches or so from his chest—"gazongas out to here."

"Well dressed?"

"Not as if she had money, no."

So what did this mean? And did it have anything to do with Fentress' trip to the Russian River and the shootings in Floyd Mears' cabin?

8

Pete Retzyck lived with his wife in a small, somewhat dilapidated old house on Persia Street. He was home, working inside an attached, single-car garage with the door raised. The door was what he was working on, up on a ladder doing something to the automatic opener mechanism. He was brusque at first, but when I explained that Joe Buckner had given me his address and told him the reason I was calling on him his irritation morphed into a kind of grim bewilderment and he was cooperative enough.

"I still can't believe Ray's dead," he said when he came down off the ladder. "Or how he died. Craziest damn thing I ever heard of."

"So you're in agreement with his wife and Joe Buckner."

"Damn straight." Retzyck picked up a rag, wiped grease off his hands. He was somewhat younger than Fentress and Buckner, late thirties—a lean, long-armed guy with a mop of walnut-brown hair and a nose like a bent and elongated hook. "If Ray was into anything, it wasn't buying pot or stealing it at the point of a gun."

"Why do you say 'if he was into anything,' Mr. Retzyck?"

". . . Well . . ."

"Did he give you the impression he might have something going when you saw him last week?"

Retzyck hesitated again, looked away from me and up at the opener mechanism. "Goddamn thing never has worked right," he muttered. "Sticks halfway open sometimes no matter what I do to it. You know anything about garage door openers?"

I said, "Afraid not," and then prodded him back to the subject of Ray Fentress by repeating my question.

"Ah, shit, I don't know. Ray had something on his mind, that's for sure. All revved up, couldn't seem to sit still."

"You ask him what it was?"

"Sure I did. The move to the Southwest, he says, starting a new life."

"He told you he was planning to buy a farm?"

"Yeah. What're you gonna use for money to buy a farm, I asked him. Doreen saved enough while I was away, he says, but he got kind of shifty eyed when he said it. So I pressed him a little."

"And?"

"And nothing," Retzyck said. "All he'd say was money wouldn't be a problem. But I'll tell you again, mister—whatever he was up to, it didn't have anything to do with pot or using a gun to get himself a stake. No way."

"Do you have any idea what his connection to Floyd Mears was?"

"No." Then, after a pause, "Well, there was a guy had a name something like that, met him once at this hunting camp Ray and me went to, but that was a couple of years ago."

"Where was this camp?"

"Lake County. Up by Lake Pillsbury. Good hunting in that area, plenty of blacktail deer."

Lake County and Sonoma County are contiguous, though Lake Pillsbury is a considerable distance from the Russian River resort area. A long way from the city, too. "How did you and Ray happen to go there?"

"Guy I know invited us. Old army buddy of mine, lives up that way. We keep in touch."

"You and Ray go just the one time?"

"No, twice. I think he went another time or two by himself."

"The man with the name that might've been Floyd Mears. Was he there the second time you went?"

"I'm not sure. Might've been."

"Can you describe him?"

"After two years? Besides, I'm no good at that," Retzyck said. "One face is the same as another to me. And there were maybe a dozen guys at the camp, all strangers except for Ray and my buddy Anthony."

"Did Ray spend much time with this man?"

"Can't tell you that, either. My memory of those times is pretty hazy. There was a lot of drinking when we weren't out in the woods hunting . . . you know how it is when a bunch of guys get together stag away from home."

Well, no, I didn't. Not where blood sports were involved.

"All I remember for sure," Retzyck went on, "is that I didn't nail a buck and neither did Ray, not either time we went together."

"The friend who invited you to the camp—Anthony, was it?"

"Anthony Bellini."

"Still in touch with him?"

"Sure, off and on."

"I'd like to talk to him. Would you call him, pave the way for me?"

"What, you mean now?"

"If you don't mind. You can use my cell phone."

Retzyck shrugged. "Okay, but why bother? I mean, even if it was Mears at the camp and that's how Ray knew him, what difference does it make?"

"Probably none," I said, "but I don't have much else to go on right now. That's the way my job works sometimes. Grab at any thread you can find and hope it leads you where you want to go."

"Some job."

He went into the house to get his friend's phone number, and when he came back I gave him my cell and he made the call. But Anthony Bellini wasn't answering his cell; the call went to voice mail. At my request Retzyck left a message explaining who I was and what I was after, and saying that I would make direct contact later on.

When he was done, he handed my phone back saying, "You really think you can find out why Ray got himself killed in that pot dealer's cabin? You're not just taking Doreen's money?"

"That's not how I operate. I won't take her money at all if I can't find out."

"Yeah? Freebie? How come?"

"Because I feel sorry for her—"

"Sorry don't pay bills."

"—and because I'm the one who found the bodies. I don't like loose ends, Mr. Retzyck, particularly not when I'm personally involved."

"So you're doing this for yourself as much as Doreen."

I hadn't thought of it that way before, but in a sense it was true. "Partly," I admitted, "but my clients come first. Always."

Retzyck said again, "Some job," this time with the sort of mild wonder people have for a breed they don't quite understand.

I t was Sunday morning, on my third try, before I reached Anthony Bellini. He was cooperative enough, but he didn't have much to tell me, at least not yet. He hadn't known Floyd Mears, couldn't recall if that was the name of the man who'd been at the hunting camp when Ray Fentress was there two years ago.

"I sort of remember him," Bellini said. "He wasn't a regular. One of the other guys brought him a couple of times—Sam Patterson, I think it was."

"Do you have contact information for Patterson?"

"Not where he is now. Sam got himself killed in a hunting accident up in the Sierras about a year ago."

Another reason to avoid blood sports, at least to my way of thinking. "Did he live in Sonoma County?"

"No, here in Lake County. Kelseyville. But he got around pretty good, Sam did. Knew a lot of people, brought more than a few guests to the camp. The more the merrier, that's our policy."

"Uh-huh. Anyone else in the core group who might remember the man?"

"Jason Quinones. He owns the property, started the camp years back. He'd know if anyone does."

"Would you ask him for me?"

"No problem. Give me your number; I'll get back to you."

. . .

Late afternoon when Bellini called. "The guy at the camp was Floyd Mears, all right," he said. "Jason keeps a list of everybody comes there and how often. Mears was there half a dozen times over three seasons."

"How many when Ray Fentress was also there?"

"Three, according to Jason's records."

"The last time was when?"

"Couple of years ago. Middle of May."

"Of 2014."

"Right."

Middle of May. Four weeks before Ray Fentress was arrested on the drunk driving, resisting arrest, and aggravated assault charges. If there was any significance in that, I had no idea what it could be.

"Does Jason remember whether Mears and Ray Fentress buddied up?" I asked.

"No. He says Mears kept mostly to himself."

So all I had for certain was testimony that Fentress and Mears had been in relatively close proximity on three occasions, close enough so that they'd at least had a nodding acquaintance; long weekends in the woods draw like-minded individuals together to some degree, even if they're strangers to each other at first. Which apparently explained how the two of them had met, but nothing else. If anything, it strengthened the prima facie case against Fentress as the catalyst in the double homicide.

This was how things shaped up: At the hunting camp Fentress either was told or found out some other way that Mears grew and sold marijuana. While in prison Fentress concocted a scheme to hijack pot and cash in order to finance a move to the

Southwest and the purchase of a farm; and when he got out he checked to make sure Mears was still living in the same place, then bought a Saturday night special and drove up to the Russian River to carry out the plan. Mears wasn't home, so Fentress shot the Doberman because it was the only way he could get past the animal and into the grow shed. After he looted it, he went into the cabin looking for money and more pot. Mears came home and caught him, either was armed with the .45 or had the piece stashed where he could get at it quickly, and both of them died in a hail of lead.

Added up well enough, no evident loose ends. That was how Heidegger and his superiors viewed it, and they'd be even more satisfied when I told them of the hunting camp connection.

It didn't satisfy me, though.

What was wrong with it was that it didn't fit Fentress' character. His wife, his friends, his background, couldn't all be wrong about the kind of man he'd been. Sure, he'd committed a couple of violent felonies, but they hadn't involved sober premeditation or firearms or pot or theft. And yes, prison can change a man, but seldom to such a radical degree in only eighteen months in a minimum-security lockup like Mule Creek.

So if the obvious explanation was the wrong one, I was right back to square one. Why *had* Fentress gone to see Mears that day, if not to buy or steal marijuana?

There were other nagging questions, too. Why had the dog been shot if it wasn't to get into the shed to steal weed? Where had the Saturday night special come from if Fentress hadn't brought it with him? Why had he been so sure he could lay hands on enough money to buy himself a farm? Where had he expected to get it and by what means, and did it have anything to do with Mears?

His little tête-à-tête with the unknown blonde in the Big-horn Tavern bothered me, too. Out of character again, unless she was somehow tied into his money plans. I'd told Pete Retzyck about it and asked if Fentress had said anything to him about her. No, and Retzyck didn't know any woman who answered her description. He'd also seconded Joe Buckner's declaration that Fentress never cheated on his wife—"Ray kept his dick where it belonged," was the way Retzyck put it. So unless somebody else I talked to knew who she was, I had no way of finding out.

Dead ends looming all along the line.

9

Kennedy Landscape Designs was a substantial operation that occupied an entire block, had an employee roll of more than two dozen, and serviced other nearby Peninsula communities in addition to Millbrae—San Bruno, Burlingame, San Mateo. Tamara had told me this, and a sign at the entrance corroborated it. The sign also said that it was Diamond Certified, whatever that meant, and listed its specialties: Japanese gardens, ponds and waterfalls, brick and flagstone patios and retaining walls, irrigation systems, sprinkler installation and repair, complete tree service.

It was a little before noon on Monday when I got there. I'd called ahead for an appointment with the owner, Philip Kennedy, and a good thing I had, because he was busy when I walked into the cottage-style office building and I had to wait ten minutes past the scheduled time before he was free to see me. His office might as well have been a greenhouse, as full as it was of potted ferns and schefflera and a colorful array of flowering plants I didn't recognize. Kennedy was a plump, energetic little man in his sixties; if he'd had a white beard and worn a tall red cap, given the business he was in, he'd have resembled a garden gnome.

He said, "Sorry to keep you waiting, it's been a busy morning," and pumped my hand and invited me to sit down.

I parked my hinder in a rattan chair next to a plant that had curved, fingerlike leaves—not too close, on the off-chance it was carnivorous. Instead of occupying the chair behind his desk, Kennedy sat close by in a chair similar to the one I was in. So his broad desk wouldn't be between us, I thought. The companionable type, a contributing factor, no doubt, to the success of his business.

"Ray Fentress. Such a sad case. First that trouble with the police that sent him to prison, and now . . ." Kennedy sighed and wagged his head. "I feel sorry for his wife."

"So do I. That's why I'm trying to help her."

"In what way, if you don't mind my asking? There's no question about what happened at the Russian River, is there?"

"There might be, but I'm not investigating the homicides. Couldn't if I wanted to." I told him what Doreen Fentress had hired me to do.

"Closure," he said, nodding.

"One way or another."

"You don't sound optimistic."

"Frankly, I'm not."

"Sad," Kennedy said again. He scooted his chair over to the desk, scribbled on a pad of paper. "Making a note to send her flowers," he said when he turned back to me.

Good for him. Kindhearted as well as sociable.

I asked, "Did Fentress happen to get in touch with you after he was released?"

"No, he didn't. I didn't even know he'd been released."

"No contact at all since his arrest, then."

"None."

"He was employed here seven years, is that right?"

"Sounds right. I'd have to look at the records to be sure."

"Was he part of a regular crew?"

Kennedy wagged his head again. "Ray was a jack-of-all-trades, so to speak—good at landscaping, good at tree work, good at just about everything we do. So we put him wherever he was needed, whatever project."

"Do you recall if there was an employee he was particularly friendly with?"

"I don't, no. I didn't know him well, you understand. Thirty people working for me, can't get to know them all." He sounded regretful of the fact. "But he was a good employee; I can tell you that. Always on time, hardly ever missed a day, liked working with plants, flowers, trees. Never any problems with him until the last month or so before he was arrested."

"Oh? What happened then?"

"Well, he began drinking rather heavily. Not on the job, so far as I know, but he came to work badly hungover three or four times. Missed a couple of days, too. Hal Waxman finally had to give him a shape-up-or-else warning." Another headshake. "I hate to fire a good man, but when I can't count on him anymore and his conduct reflects badly on the business . . ."

"Do you have any idea what caused the sudden binge drinking?"

"No. Something weighing on his mind, I suppose."

"You mentioned Hal Waxman. Who would he be?"

"Our yard foreman. You might talk to him."

"I'll do that. Where do I find him?"

"In the distribution center, probably. I'll phone over there and tell him you're coming."

Distribution center was a polite term for *warehouse,* the largest of the three buildings on the lot. It was crammed with all sorts of landscaping materials and machinery that included rototillers, backhoes, John Deere Gators. A greenhouse attached to the rear was lush with plants, every kind from the bedding variety of flowers to large shrubs, and multiple varieties and sizes of trees in tubs.

Hal Waxman was waiting for me at the open entrance doors. The yard foreman looked to be in his early forties, a pear-shaped man with a matching pear-shaped face—narrow at the brow, somewhat broad across the cheeks and jawline. He wore a pair of green overalls with *Kennedy Landscaping Designs* stitched over the breast pocket, had a clipboard in one hand and an empty black-bowled briar pipe clamped between his teeth.

He saw me looking at the pipe while we shook hands. "I quit smoking fifteen years ago," he said a little ruefully, "but I can't get out of the habit of chewing on the stem."

"I'm an ex-smoker myself. Coffin nails, to my everlasting regret."

"Yeah. You still get cravings?"

"Not in a long time."

"I do, but only after a big meal. Well. The boss said you wanted to ask me about Ray Fentress?"

"About the last month he was employed here, yes."

"Uh-huh. Before he started boozing and his life went to hell. Damn shame. Nice guy, steady, no trouble until then."

"You have any idea what happened to change him?"

"No," Waxman said. "I asked him straight out the morning he came in still half in the bag, but he wouldn't talk about it. Whatever it was, it was eating hell out of him."

"When exactly did it start, do you remember?"

He worked his memory, gnawing audibly on the pipe stem like a dog worrying a stick. "While we were doing a major relandscaping job at the Holloway estate in Burlingame. Fountains, waterfalls, flagstone paths, you name it."

"Fentress worked on that job?"

"From the first. About three months."

"Did anything happen during that period that might explain his sudden drinking?"

"Not that I know of. Everything went real smooth, no problems. Well, except for the Holloways' young daughter, but her behavior didn't have anything to do with Ray."

"Behavior?"

"She liked to parade around in a bikini, her and some of her friends, and flirt with the crew." Waxman shook his head disapprovingly. "Spoiled rich kid. If she were my kid, I wouldn't have put up with it."

"Just harmless flirting, then?"

"Well, none of the men said otherwise. Or seemed to mind except when she followed them around and got in their way. Maybe she was the reason for the stop-work order, but I don't see how, since nobody here complained about her."

"Stop-work order?"

"Mr. Holloway called it in when we had less than three weeks left on the job. No workmen allowed on the property until further notice."

"He didn't give a reason?"

"Nope. Just the order. Then a couple weeks later, somebody

in his office calls up and says okay, now we can go ahead and finish up."

I chewed on that before I said, "Can you tell me exactly when the stop-work order was issued?"

"Must've been the middle of June," Waxman said. "I remember because it was right after the Fourth of July that the crew went back to work."

"Middle of June. Just about the time Ray Fentress was arrested."

"Say, that's right. Day or two afterward, I think it was. But that couldn't've had anything to do with Ray or his boozing. I mean, I don't see how it could, do you?"

"No," I said, "I don't."

Coincidence, probably, I was thinking as I returned to my car. Puzzling, but irrelevant. Even if there'd been some sort of personal connection between Fentress and the Holloway family that had triggered the change in him, it had all happened nearly two years ago; a connection, after all that time, to the double shooting at Floyd Mears' cabin seemed inconceivable.

And yet . . .

I've had stranger cases, a few with such seemingly disjointed facts as these that turned out to be interrelated after all. This one was a muddle no matter what linked up and what didn't, and I was fresh out of other leads to help untangle it. Unless I wanted to report failure to Doreen Fentress and walk away from the investigation—and I was not ready to do that just yet—I owed it to her and to myself to explore even the most tenuous possibilities.

10

When I got back to South Park, the noise level from the renovation work on the three-quarter-acre oval seemed even louder than usual. The clamor, continual when the weather permitted, penetrated the old walls of our building and made conducting business a literal headache at times. Not that Tamara or I begrudged the necessity for it; on the contrary. The "town square of Multimedia Gulch," smack in the middle of SoMa and its technology ecosystem, had become something of an eyesore in recent years—dead grass, cracked asphalt paths, sycamores and elms in poor shape, the creosote-covered children's play structures so dilapidated the city had finally removed them, leaving a sandy pit that had devolved into a dog run. Finally a group of residents and businesses, ours included, had gotten together and spearheaded the renovation, the first in more than forty years. When it was finished, South Park would have wider pathways, open meadows and raised grass hillocks, plazas, concrete retaining walls with benches, and a new kids' play area. The sooner the better, for more reasons than one.

In the office I asked Tamara to find out anything that might be even remotely relevant about the Holloways of Burlingame. She was busy with other, more pressing work, so it took a while for her to accommodate the request.

"I pulled up some interesting bits," she said when she called me into her office. "Might be worth looking into."

"Such as?"

"Let me give you a little background on the Holloways first. The family head, Vernon, is a near one-percenter—not Silicon Valley mega-rich, but worth around twenty mil on paper. Venture capital profits. Has a rep as a cutthroat businessman."

"Cutthroat meaning what? Honestly aggressive, or one of the fast and loose players?"

"None of those dudes ever got where they are without their share of dirty tricks."

"Any specifics I should know about?"

"Well, Holloway's clean enough on the surface. No ties to illegal activities, never the subject of any kind of investigation." Tamara consulted her computer screen. "Owns the estate in Burlingame outright, bought it eleven years ago for four mil. Pays his taxes on time, what little bite there is after his accountants finish finding all the loopholes. Donates to half a dozen charities. Pays alimony to two of his three ex-wives—off the money hook with the third because she found herself an even richer sugar daddy."

"What about his daughter?"

"Melanie Joy. Some name, huh? Only child—only one he'll admit to anyway. Man also has a rep as a pussy hound."

I let that pass. "How old is Melanie Joy?"

"Twenty-four. Still living with Daddy on the Burlingame estate. Real wild child for a while. Social media postings full of hints and outright declarations about sex, drugs, and gambling. But all that changed about eighteen months ago."

"Changed how?"

"This is where it gets interesting. No posts on her active site accounts for over a week, then they were all shut down and stayed that way for nearly three months. Her new Facebook and Twitter accounts are nothing like the old ones, no mention of the stuff she was into before, mostly photos and chit-chat about this conservative stockbroker she's been dating. Wild to mild."

"What caused the sudden turnaround?"

"No definite answer. Whatever it was, it's been kept private. I couldn't pick up a whisper anywhere."

"When exactly was her old account shut down?"

"End of June 2014."

"Not long after Ray Fentress got himself arrested and Vernon Holloway issued his stop-work order to Kennedy Landscape Designs."

"Yup."

"Could be coincidence," I said. "There's nothing that ties Fentress to the Holloway girl except that they were both on the estate grounds while he was working there. And nothing that ties either of them to what happened at Floyd Mears' cabin."

"No, but there's a Melanie Joy tie to Sonoma County."

"Oh?"

"Girl was heavy into gambling until that summer," Tamara said. "Roulette, baccarat, just about any big-action game. Vegas once in a while, but mostly she favored Indian casinos closer to home. Her number one hangout was the Graton Resort and Casino in Rohnert Park. Used to go up there weekends, sometimes with her former boyfriend, sometimes with girl-friends, sometimes by herself."

Rohnert Park is less than fifty miles north of San Francisco, seventy-five or so north of Burlingame—an easy round-trip drive. It's also not much more than half an hour from the Russian River resort area.

Tamara said, "Meaningful, you think?"

"I don't know. Could be just another coincidence."

"You always advised me not to trust coincidences when they come in bunches."

"True enough, but not trusting them doesn't mean they don't happen now and then. I just don't see how all these links could tie together, where they'd lead if they do."

"Real puzzle, all right."

I ruminated for a time. "The Graton Casino," I said then. "Vegas-style glitter palace, isn't it? Attractive to high rollers?"

"Right. Largest resort casino west of Vegas. Built by the Federated Indians of the Graton Rancheria, opened in 2013—I looked up their website." Tamara tapped a couple of keys, peered at her monitor again. "Six-hundred-seat Events Center, conference rooms, a dozen restaurants, and what they call a high-energy casino floor—three thousand slots, hundred forty-four table games, live poker room, VIP gaming salons."

The kind of place they'd have had to drag me into kicking and screaming. "You said Melanie Holloway liked high-stakes games. Did she win or lose large amounts?"

"Can't be sure without more checking. Seems like she lost more than she won, though."

"So if she was dropping large chunks, her father might've put a stop to it, laid down the law. That could be the reason, or part of the reason, for the sudden turnaround in her life-style."

"Could," Tamara agreed.

"Then again," I said, "something may have happened during the last of her gambling weekends that brought about the sudden change. Is there any way of finding out if she went to the Graton Casino right before her social media silence?"

"Not on the Net. But if you want to take a shot at it, there might be another way."

"And that is?"

"Melanie Joy's former good-time boyfriend was pissed about being dumped. Some Twitter and Facebook grumbles to that effect. Dude might've had his eye on the Holloway fortune—he's not one of the rich crowd—and Papa pressured Melanie to break it off. Or maybe they had a hassle that last weekend and she's the one who ended it. Anyhow, he might know something and be willing to talk about it."

"Name?"

"Conner Jacklin. He's a physical terrorist."

"A *what*?"

Tamara let me see one of her impish grins. "My name for dudes in his profession. Never let one of 'em torture me."

"Uh-huh. Physical therapist, you mean."

"Right. Does his thing in a Burlingame health club, the EverYoung Fitness Center. That's where Melanie Joy hooked up with him—he was her personal trainer."

11

The EverYoung Fitness Center, according to the advertisements printed on its long front window, was a "full-service health spa for men and women of all ages." It was on a side street off Burlingame Avenue, in the Peninsula community's downtown shopping district. You could tell from its size and its ornate old-fashioned brick façade that it catered to the area's more affluent citizens. Visible through a long front window were eight or nine individuals of both sexes busily and sweatily exercising on a long row of expensive-looking treadmills.

A smiling young woman, the picture of rosy-cheeked and trim-bodied health, presided over a desk in the open lobby. I gave her my name and she checked her computer to confirm that I had an eleven-thirty appointment with Conner Jacklin. He was with a client at the moment, she informed me, and might be a bit late. But definitely not more than five or ten minutes, she said brightly. Was I personally acquainted with Mr. Jacklin or had he been recommended to me? Recommended, I said, by a friend of Melanie Joy Holloway. Her smile dimmed for an instant, like the flicker of a lamp before a power outage, and then brightened again. Knows Melanie Joy, I thought, and doesn't like her much if at all.

The young woman invited me to have a seat, handed me one of EverYoung's brochures to read while I waited. I sat in a comfortable, formfitting chair and glanced through the brochure. Their personal trainers were NCSF and ACE certified, acronyms that meant nothing to me, and provided individualized exercise programs that included strength training, aerobic and anaerobic training, cardiovascular and spinal care, and therapeutic massage. The club also featured such state-of-the-art exercise equipment as total body elliptical crosstrainers, Life Fitness Lifecycles, incline and decline mountain climber treadmills, and upright and recumbent bikes. Altogether it sounded pretty healthful, all right, but it also sounded like a hell of a lot of hard work. Well, no pain, no gain, as they say.

True to the receptionist's word, Conner Jacklin was less than ten minutes late for our appointment. He came out of an area at the rear filled with more customers sweating away on total body elliptical crosstrainers and the like, greeted me with a professional smile and a hearty handshake, and managed not to look disapproving as he eyed my somewhat expansive midsection. He was also the picture of twentysomething health, of course, in a pair of white ducks and a tight white T-shirt. You could have used the word *Adonis* to describe him with some justification. Sculpted body with bulging pecs and biceps, blond hair cut short, blue eyes, and chiseled features. Just the type of stud a young, hot-blooded rich girl would find irresistible.

He didn't seem quite so perfect to me, however. Maybe it was a male jealousy thing, but I didn't like him on sight. There was a shine in his blue-eyed gaze, a self-satisfied set to his mouth and jaw, the suggestion of a swagger in his manner even when he was standing still—all indicators, to my professional eye, that he was full of himself, none too intelligent, and the possessor of predatory instincts.

He said it was a pleasure to meet me, which was probably a lie, and welcomed me to EverYoung with a little programmed speech about helping to achieve whatever my personal goals might be. After which he asked the same question the young woman at the desk had asked. I looked him straight in the eye and gave him the same answer.

His reaction to Melanie Joy Holloway's name was to lose the smile, his lips pulling into a tight line. I watched him struggle to regain his professional composure, then prodded him off balance again by saying, "She's the reason I'm here, but it's not to sign up for an exercise program. I have a few questions about your relationship with her."

"Why? What for? Who're you?"

I let him see the photostat of my license. The confused look on his handsome face confirmed my opinion of his mental acuity. "What the hell?" he said in a lowered voice. "I haven't seen Mel in more than a year. You want the truth, I hope I never see her again."

"Is there someplace private we can talk?"

". . . Huh?"

"Too public out here, wouldn't you say?"

"I just told you—" He wagged his head as if to clear it. The young woman at the desk was watching us; Jacklin saw that, too, and it made up his mind for him. "Yeah, okay. Follow me."

I trailed him into the rear of the building, through the weight and exercise room, and through an open door. Massage room: metal table, towels on racks, glass-doored cabinet full of emoluments, curtained alcove for changing in privacy. The mingled smells of body oils, disinfectant, and stale sweat assumed miasmic proportions when Jacklin shut the door.

"Listen," he said, turning toward me, "if that bitch is in trouble again, you're talking to the wrong guy. I don't know anything about it."

"Bitch, Mr. Jacklin?"

"You heard me right. Bitch plain and simple."

"Was she in some kind of trouble when the two of you were together?"

"What?"

"In trouble again, you said. Again."

"Mel was always in some kind of trouble back then."

"What kind, specifically? With the law?"

"Nah, nothing like that." He gnawed on his lower lip with the sort of bright white teeth you see in dental ads. "What's this all about, anyway? You working for Melanie's father or something?"

"I can't tell you that. Privileged information."

"Yeah, well, it's going on two years since I laid eyes on her. I don't get how what happened that long ago has to do with me."

"Probably nothing," I said. "I'm just gathering information. Which one of you broke off your relationship?"

A little silence. Then he lifted and lowered a shoulder and said, "It sure as hell wasn't my idea. I thought we were tight, real tight."

"The kind of tight that could lead to marriage?"

"Yeah, maybe. So?" Jacklin said sullenly. "She kept throwing out signals, telling me she loved me every time we got it on together. Then all of a sudden . . . boom, good-bye, Conner. No explanation, nothing. Pretended I didn't exist after she came back from wherever she disappeared to."

"Disappeared? When was that?"

"Summer. Early summer."

"Middle of June?"

"Around then, yeah."

"For how long?"

"Week, two weeks, I don't remember exactly."

"Any idea where she might've been all that time?"

"No." Jacklin went to lean against the massage table, his hands gripping its beveled edge. "But I figure maybe she hooked up with some guy and shacked up with him somewhere for a week or two. I wouldn't put it past her the way she was then."

"Uh-huh."

"And then something heavy must've happened. The guy beat her up or got her wasted on crystal meth or something and she ended up in jail or the hospital for a week or two. That'd explain it, right?"

"It might."

"But not the rest of it. Why she dumped me and quit dealing with her old friends."

I asked, "When did you last see her?"

"Right before she disappeared. She was gonna spend the weekend at this Indian casino up north."

"The Graton in Rohnert Park?"

"Yeah. How'd you know that?"

"You didn't go with her?"

"No. I had a private session that Saturday." The near smirk that crossed Jacklin's mouth told me the "private session" had had little or nothing to do with personal fitness training.

"Did she go with anybody else?"

"Not that I know of. She wanted us to make a weekend of it. Pissed when I begged off."

"Did she often go to the Graton Casino by herself?"

"Now and then. She had a thing for the place. Didn't matter to her if anybody was with her or not. All she wanted to do was gamble, park her ass at a roulette or baccarat table for hours at a stretch. Not me, man. Waste of time and money."

"Make large bets, did she?"

"Yeah, sometimes, if she hit a winning streak. Not that that happened very often."

"How large?"

"Biggest single bet I ever saw her make was five hundred."

"Did she ever win big?"

"Nah. A couple grand once at baccarat, but she blew it all the next day."

"So she lost more often than she won."

"Got that right. Tossed away dollars like they were pennies."

"How heavy were her losses?"

"Thousands sometimes. Eight K once when I wasn't with her. Didn't bother her." Jacklin's mouth twisted into a bitter little sneer. "Why should it? Her old man's rich as hell."

"Did he know how much she was losing?"

"Sure, he knew. Kept after her to quit, threatened to cut her off if she didn't cool it."

"Maybe he finally got through to her," I said. "Maybe that's the reason, or part of the reason, she altered her lifestyle."

"No way," Jacklin said. "Mel never paid any attention to her old man when I knew her, just went ahead and did what she wanted and bragged about it afterward. He was just blowing smoke with his threats." The sneer again. "Daddy's baby girl and she knew it."

"Then how do you account for the change in her?"

"I can't, man. Neither can anybody else. She blew off all her chick friends the same time she did me, wouldn't tell anybody why. Holloway wouldn't tell me, either."

"You spoke to him?"

"Once, for about five minutes, and he did all the talking."

"When was that?"

"After she came back home from wherever she disappeared to." The bitterness was palpable in Jacklin's voice now. "Showed up here one day, said Mel was through with me and if I knew what was good for me I'd never try to see her again. Prick even waved a check in my face. Five thousand bucks, for Christ's sake, like he was firing me from some fucking job."

"And you turned it down?"

"Like hell I did. I was entitled to something after what the bitch did to me, wasn't I? Even a lousy five K to sign a paper promising I'd never have anything to do with her again?"

On the way back to the city, I made an effort to put what I'd learned from Conner Jacklin together with the other bits and pieces into a credible scenario that would explain Melanie Holloway's brief disappearance and its aftermath. Jacklin's theory of a pickup who'd physically abused her and/or fed her heavy doses of hard drugs was reasonable enough. A couple of weeks in jail or a hospital somewhere would explain the disappearance, all right. The hush-up afterward, too; Vernon Holloway was the type to take whatever steps necessary to avoid negative publicity for himself and his reckless daughter. It might also explain Melanie's lifestyle change, whether Jacklin thought so or not. The experience, if it was a bad one, could have scared the hell out of her and made Holloway finally lay down the law.

But if that was the answer, then I was looking at another dead end as far as Ray Fentress was concerned. He hadn't been the type to appeal to a then-twenty-two-year-old rich girl; neither had Floyd Mears. Which reduced the slim links between Fentress and Melanie Holloway to a couple of coincidences after all.

Well, suppose Jacklin's theory was only half-right. Suppose Melanie hadn't hooked up with another man that weekend. Suppose her gambler's luck had changed and she'd finally hit a big-time winning streak; that she was carrying a large amount of cash when she left the casino; that she'd been accosted in the parking lot or followed somewhere . . . mugged, robbed, hurt badly enough in the process to wind up in the hospital. There had been no police report of such an incident or Tamara would have turned it up, but the girl could have insisted her father be notified instead of the cops. The rest of the scenario— the hush-up, Melanie incommunicado, the lifestyle change— would then follow the same explanatory lines.

And suppose the perps were Floyd Mears and Ray Fentress. Mears the instigator, Fentress a reluctant accomplice. The crime wouldn't have been premeditated; Fentress could have known of Melanie's weekend plans, but not that she'd win a large sum of money. Spur-of-the-moment thing. Okay, but why would the two of them be at the Graton Casino that night? Fentress hadn't been a gambler, or his widow or one of the people I'd talked to would have mentioned it. Well, assuming he and Mears had buddied up at the Lake County hunting camp, maybe they'd decided to get together at the casino, have a few drinks, and look the place over . . . boys' night out. And while they were there Fentress recognized Melanie Holloway while she was on her winning streak, Mears hatched the robbery idea and talked Fentress into it—

No, dammit, it didn't feel right, didn't hang together. You could poke a bunch of holes in it without half-trying.

Even if Melanie had hit a hot streak, her total winnings couldn't have amounted to much more than ten thousand dollars; by law casinos have to report winnings above that amount to the IRS, and if she'd insisted on taking the money in cash they would have insisted in return on providing a security escort when she left the casino. If a robbery had been managed and Fentress had gotten his share and stashed it somewhere, he'd have had no reason to go calling on Mears after his release from prison; he and his wife could've just packed up and moved immediately. And if he hadn't gotten his share and was worried that Mears would try to cheat him out of it, it was as out of character for him to threaten Mears with a gun for a few thousand dollars in cash as it was for a few hundred worth of marijuana—not nearly enough money to put a down payment on a farm, much less buy one.

Two other things didn't fit, either. The fact that whatever had been preying on Fentress's mind had started him drinking heavily in June of 2014, a month before Melanie Holloway's disappearance. And the recent presence of the mystery woman named Mary.

Robbery wasn't the answer.

12

The house Doreen Fentress had shared with her late husband was a small frame that dated back to the postwar forties, its roof and off-white paint job showing signs of neglect. No garage. A tiny front yard of weed-riddled grass bordered by flower beds and decorated with an ancient, chipped garden statue of what might have been a cherub holding a bowl filled with ferns and yellow jonquils (I knew that's what they were because jonquils are among Kerry's favorite flowers). Mrs. Fentress had apparently done what she could to keep up appearances, but working two jobs wouldn't have left her much time or energy for yardwork.

At one time you probably could have bought the property for under ten thousand dollars; now, given San Francisco's ever-increasing real estate prices and the Excelsior next in line to the Mission District for gentrification, it would go for upward of five hundred thousand. No wonder longtime residents have begun to sell out and move away in droves, deeding over much of the city to the affluent. If the Fentresses had owned the place, they could have put it on the market and made a bundle to finance Ray Fentress' dream of owning a farm. But it was a rental they'd occupied for fifteen years. The owner, unlike most landlords, wasn't greedy; he kept the monthly nut affordable and evidently had no inclination to sell. Doreen Fentress would be able to continue living there in the short run, at least.

It was a little after four when I arrived at the house. The widow had told me at our first meeting that she'd been given some time off from her clerk's job, and I'd called to make sure she was home before I drove out. She must have been watching for me from behind the curtained front window; the door opened before I was halfway up the cracked front path. A small black-and-white wire-haired terrier came out with her and sat peeking around one of her legs, like a kid hiding behind his mother's skirts.

I tend to be wary of dogs, no matter what size; I've had run-ins with more than one breed, including a scary one not so long ago that had come close to being fatal. My expression as I glanced down at the terrier must have alerted Mrs. Fentress, because she said, "Don't worry, she won't bite. Tina's a sweet dog, just very shy. Aren't you, Tina?" Mrs. Fentress reached down to pat the animal's head affectionately. It licked her hand in return.

The three of us went inside, Tina giving me a wide berth. Mrs. Fentress seemed more composed today, her pale skin less waxy and the aura of melancholy less pronounced—partly, I thought, because this interview was being conducted in familiar surroundings instead of a stranger's office. She led me into a tidy living room that had a faint doggy odor beneath a liberal spraying of lemon-scented air freshener.

The room was sparsely furnished: two old-fashioned Morris chairs sided by floor lamps, a mismatched two-seat couch, a couple of end tables, and a sideboard of a darker-colored wood. Much if not all of it had probably come with the house. All the lamps and a ceiling globe were on, making the room very bright. Light to chase away more than one kind of darkness.

A pillowed basket bed sat next to the chair that was obviously Mrs. Fentress'; the dog jumped into it, put her head on her paws, and watched me with eyes that were as sad as her owner's. The placement of the basket and the maternal way the woman talked to the dog was another attempt at keeping darkness at bay, I thought, the kind engendered by both childlessness and loneliness.

I declined the ritual offer of something to drink, and we sat down. I'd told her on the phone that I had a preliminary report for her and some questions to ask; I could have done both over the wire, but it seemed kinder to see her in person. Besides, I had another reason for coming to the house.

She sat quietly, one hand stretched down to fondle the terrier's ears, while I told her the probable way in which her husband had come to know Floyd Mears. I finished by saying, "But I'm afraid that only raises more questions. Did your husband ever say anything to you about his trips to the hunting camp, the people he met there?"

"Very little. Hunting, even when he brought home venison . . . well, that's one interest we didn't share."

"No mention of having made a new friend?"

"No. Not that I remember."

"Did he keep a list of names and telephone numbers? Here at home, I mean."

"An address book? I don't think so, no. I never saw one."

"Where did he keep his personal papers?"

"In the desk in the dining room. But I went through every-thing before I came to see you. There's nothing new there, just his insurance policy and birth certificate, old hunting licenses, things like that."

"Letters, postcards, notes of any kind?"

"No."

"What about files of paid bills and bank statements from eighteen months ago? Do you still have those?"

"Yes. In a box in the spare bedroom closet."

"Did he pay the monthly bills back then or did you?"

"I did. Ray had no head for figures."

"Do you remember anything unusual that caught your eye during the month before his arrest? An unfamiliar credit card charge, for instance."

"No."

"Would it be all right if I had a look at the paperwork from that period?"

The skin between her eyes and across her forehead pinched together. "I suppose so. But why?"

"I've been told your husband began drinking heavily around that time. That's true, isn't it?"

". . . Yes. But I don't see—"

"He was a moderate drinker before that, just a few beers now and then according to Joe Buckner and Pete Retzyck. Do you have any idea what led to the heavy drinking?"

"No. He wouldn't talk about it."

"How would you describe him during that month? Upset, worried, nervous, secretive?"

"Withdrawn most of the time," Mrs. Fentress said. Memory caused her fingers to tighten on Tina's ruff, the terrier to whimper in response. "When he did talk, it was about moving away, starting over. Once he said we ought to move right away, but he knew we couldn't afford it. We were swamped with bills— we couldn't just pack up and leave."

"At that time he was working on a large estate in Burlingame, a lengthy relandscaping job for a man named Vernon Holloway. Did he say anything about that?"

She thought for a time before she said, "The job at first, yes. He was impressed by the property, the new landscaping plans."

"At first, you said. But not during that last month?"

". . . Not that I remember."

"Vernon Holloway has a daughter named Melanie Joy, twenty-two at the time. Did he ever mention her?"

"Yes, once or twice. He said she and her friends were spoiled rich kids . . . running around half-naked, bothering the crew. . . ." Her forehead wrinkled again. "You're not implying the girl had anything to do with Ray's drinking? That he made a pass at her and she rejected him?"

"No. Just asking questions, trying to fit pieces together."

"Well, that's not one you should consider," she said. "Ray had his vices, God knows, but he wasn't a chaser and he was twice that girl's age."

Which meant nothing, necessarily. The number of faithful middle-aged husbands who lost their heads over younger women is legion. But there was no gain in reminding Mrs. Fentress of the fact. There wouldn't be any, either, in mentioning her husband's afternoon tête-à-tête with the woman named Mary at the Bighorn Tavern; it was unlikely Mrs. Fentress knew who Mary was, and I had no desire to rub salt in the open wound of her grief.

I said, "Was gambling one of his vices, Mrs. Fentress?"

She blinked at the abrupt shift in questions. "Gambling? Ray? No, never."

"So he had no interest that you know about in Indian casinos, such as the fancy new one in Sonoma County—the Graton Resort and Casino?"

"My God, no. What does that place have to do with Ray?"

"Probably nothing. Just a possibility that came up."

The terrier uncurled out of the basket, put forepaws on Mrs. Fentress's knees—begging for attention. She picked the dog up, cradled and cuddled her against her breast. "I don't understand all these questions. Why are you so interested in what happened the month before Ray went to prison? What does that have to do with his murder?"

"I don't know that it has anything to do with it. Trying to fit pieces together, as I said." I got to my feet. "Could I have a look at those stored files now?"

She said, "Yes, all right," and stood with Tina still cradled in her arms. The spare bedroom, at the rear of the house, was not much larger than a cell; a double bed, one nightstand, a bureau, and an old rocking chair left so little room that Mrs. Fentress stood in the doorway while I located the file box labeled "2014" and liberated it from the tiny closet. I deposited the box on the bed, sat down next to it for the search.

Easy task, because everything in the box was segregated in neatly labeled manila folders. I examined the credit card bills first, paying particular attention to those for May and June. The charges were all standard and all relatively small; the modest credit limits on both cards, Visa and MasterCard, had almost but not quite been maxed out and the monthly payments had been the minimum. Canceled checks and bank statements next. The largest monthly balance at any time during the year was six hundred dollars, the largest check amounts for the house rent and credit card payments. No checks made out to individuals and only a couple to cash for fifty dollars apiece. No correspondence addressed to or written by Ray Fentress. Nothing that even remotely pertained to Floyd Mears or the Holloway family.

Mrs. Fentress was still standing in the doorway with the dog in her arms, watching. She knew from my silence that I had not found anything useful; she remained silent herself as I replaced everything in the file box, returned it to the closet.

I said then, "Have you sorted through your husband's possessions, Mrs. Fentress?"

"His possessions? I don't—"

"The clothing he wore the week after he came home from Mule Creek. Whatever he might have had that he didn't take with him to the Russian River—keys, another wallet, that sort of thing."

"No. No, I . . . I couldn't bring myself . . ."

"I understand. Would you mind if I looked through them?"

She didn't mind. We went into the master bedroom, larger, with a bronze crucifix on the wall above the double bed, two cretonne chairs, and two blond-wood bureaus; the extra furniture made it seem just as cramped as the spare bedroom. She pointed out which bureau had belonged to her husband—not that it was necessary, because a man's catchall tray and two bottles of cologne sat atop it—and then stood back in the doorway as she had before to watch me, the dog as placid as a sleeping baby in her arms.

The tray held a quarter, two dimes, and four pennies, a ballpoint pen, nail clippers, an outmoded tie clip that probably hadn't been used in years. The drawers contained the usual array of underwear, socks, a pair of pajamas. I closed the last one, went to open the closet. The clothing on hangers was divided into about equal halves, his and hers. Two small suitcases on a shelf, shoes on a pair of racks, and a cased rifle and a well-used camper's rucksack tucked into one corner.

"The brown checked sport coat," Mrs. Fentress said. "Ray wore that one the day when he went to see Joe Buckner. And the jacket with the hood he wore another day when it was raining."

The slash pockets in the jacket were empty, but there was something shoved down inside the sport coat's right-side pocket. Crumpled piece of white paper, torn across at one end—the kind that comes off a small notepad. I smoothed it out. Scrawled in soft-lead pencil in a nearly illegible hand was what appeared to be an address: 357 or 557 Old Wood or Old Hood Rd. After that were the initials *MR* and, on another line, "7:00 Mon." The address number and street name were finger smudged so that I couldn't be sure.

Mrs. Fentress had come over next to me. I held the paper out so she could read it. "Mean anything to you?"

". . . No."

"Your husband's handwriting?"

"Yes."

"The sport coat. Was it dry-cleaned and then stored in the closet while he was in prison?"

"Yes, that's right."

So he must have pocketed the paper the one time he'd worn the coat last week. And the occasion hadn't been to see Joe Buckner, I was thinking; it had been the day he'd met with the woman named Mary.

"Old Wood Road," Mrs. Fentress said. She was still peering at the paper. "I have no idea where that is."

Sonoma County, the Russian River resort area. MR. Mary something? Or the name of a town—Monte Rio?

"Are you sure that's a *W* and not an *H*?" I asked her.

"I think so. Ray always wrote such a poor hand."

"What about the numbers? Three-five-seven or five-five-seven?"

"The first one looks like a five. Five-five-seven."

"I'll keep this if it's all right with you."

"Yes, of course."

With my pen I wrote "557" and "Wood" below the smudged address, then folded the paper and slipped it inside my notebook.

There was nothing else for me to look at, and no more questions to ask Mrs. Fentress. The atmosphere in the small house, with its odors of lemon and dog, its almost palpable aura of grief and loneliness and shattered lives, had grown oppressive. It made me eager to get out of there, which I did as quickly as I could manage it.

It also made me even more determined to stay with this investigation as long as I possibly could. I seemed to be the only one besides Tina capable of giving Doreen Fentress something to make her empty life just a little more tolerable.

13

I gave Tamara the paper from Ray Fentress' jacket as soon as I came into the agency the next morning. While she was running a trace on the address, I put in a call to Lieutenant Heidegger at the Sonoma County sheriff's department. He wasn't in, and the officer I spoke to didn't know when Heidegger would return. Just as well. I really had nothing definite to report that he needed to know. Courtesy call, more than anything else at this point, to maintain the cordial relationship.

It was another fifteen minutes before Tamara came into my office, a little longer than it usually takes her to track down a location. "It's Monte Rio, all right," she said. "Five-five-seven Old Wood Road. Single occupant, a woman named Marie Seldon."

"Marie, not Mary?"

"Definitely Marie."

So either Joe Buckner had misheard the blonde's name or Fentress had deliberately mispronounced it.

"Ties to Floyd Mears as well as to Fentress," Tamara said. "She's the girlfriend Mears beat up five months ago. One of her neighbors heard them fighting and called the law when she started screaming. She had to have medical attention but still refused to file a complaint."

"She stay with him after that?"

"If she did, she's crazy. Any man smacked me around, I'd dump him faster than a sack of garbage."

"How long were she and Mears hooked up?"

"Three years, according to the sheriff's report."

"So they were together when Fentress got himself in trouble with the law," I said. "It's probable he met her through Mears."

"Right."

"And if she broke up with Mears after the beating, it seems unlikely she was acting as an intermediary for him when she and Fentress got together last week."

"Unless they got back together again. No record of it, if so."

"In any event, who arranged the meeting, her or Fentress? And why? Another thing: Monday was the day of the shootings and seven p.m. could've been the time of the meeting at Mears' cabin. But then why did he have her home address written down?"

"You could ask her, see what she has to say. Or notify Lieutenant Heidegger and let him talk to her."

I thought it over. "Better me at this point," I decided. "The connections are still too tenuous to have any direct bearing on the official version of what happened at the cabin. If I can't get anything out of Seldon, then I'll go to Heidegger."

"Long drive up to Monte Rio."

"I don't have anything better to do today. There anything else I should know about Seldon before I leave?"

The answer to that was nothing much. Born in Cloverdale;

married a Guerneville resident at eighteen and moved there with him; stayed in the Russian River area after they were divorced five years later. No children. Clean slate as far as any other encounters with the law went. Employed for the past three years at a place called Millie's Gifts and Sportswear in Guerneville. Maintained a low profile for personal or financial reasons: no social media or e-mail accounts. No phone company account, either; if she used a cell phone, it was one of those prepaid jobs.

Tamara said, "There is one other thing I found out—not about Seldon, about Vernon Holloway. Might mean something, might not. Right around the time Melanie Joy disappeared, he sold off a chunk of his stock holdings—fast, over a couple of days. Strapped for ready cash, evidently, and in need of a large wad."

"How large?"

"Six figures."

"Why did he need so much cash in a hurry?"

"That I couldn't find out. Might've been an under-the-table business deal, the kind that doesn't leave a paper trail. Some of these rich dudes operate that way when they figure they can get away with it."

"Does Holloway have a history of that kind of dealing?"

"Hard to tell for sure without some major hacking, the quasi-legal kind. If he played that game before, it was spread out over a longer period of time. Easier for his accountants to cover it up that way."

"So his need for cash could've had something to do with his daughter," I said. "But not to pay off gambling debts. No casino in the world would allow a twenty-two-year-old to run up six figures' worth of losses, no matter what her pedigree."

"How else could it tie in?"

"To her? To Fentress and Mears?" I shook my head. "Maybe I can get a clue from Marie Seldon."

On the drive north across the Golden Gate Bridge, I tried again to make some cohesive sense of what I'd learned so far. I went over all the pieces, one by one. At first I couldn't put them together to form a pattern, but the more I shuffled them around, the more they began to interlock. Not all, but enough to shape an outline.

I played around with the idea all the way to the Russian River, shuffling and reshuffling, finding holes the way I had with the robbery theory and then either filling or discounting them. The upshot of all the mental gymnastics was a concept that was credible, if complicated and grim and not a little cold-blooded. I did not have enough information yet to be sure, but if the answers to a few more questions jigsawed into the pattern then I'd know.

I half-hoped I was wrong in my figuring. If I was on the right track, it would make Heidegger and some other people happy, but not me.

And not Doreen Fentress.

It was raining in Guerneville. The day had been overcast and dry in the city, but up here in redwood country there was more precipitation because most coastal storms, light and heavy both, came in off the Pacific or down from Canada and Alaska. Sixty-plus miles made a considerable difference in weather patterns, inclement and clement.

The cloud ceiling hung low, the downpour light but steady, so that the riverside community seemed to be huddled bleakly under a wet gray blanket. There wasn't much traffic and I had no trouble finding Millie's Gifts and Sportswear; the shop was on River Road, just beyond the turnoff that led to Armstrong Redwoods State Natural Reserve, in an old building with a prominent sign above the entrance.

There was a parking place a couple of doors down, a good thing, because I hadn't brought an umbrella. The shop was open, testimony to the owner's optimistic nature; at this time of year and in weather like this there weren't going to be many customers interested in local arts and crafts and an array of inexpensive sportswear, T-shirts and sweatshirts, and low-end gift items. The only person present when I walked in was a middle-aged woman with a hairdo so weird, at least in my experience, that I couldn't help staring at it. Short, lemony-blond hair topped by a pelt of shoe-polish-black hair, so that it looked as though some sort of amoebalike creature was clinging to the crown of her head.

The woman was so pleased to see a potential customer that she either didn't notice or ignored my impolite stare. "Hello," she said through a not very bright smile. "May I help you, sir?"

I dragged my gaze away from the creature and fixed it on a pair of squinty brown eyes. "I hope so," I said. "I'm looking for Marie Seldon."

The question turned her smile upside down, produced a half-resigned, half-annoyed sigh. "Oh. Well. You wouldn't be a friend or relative of hers, would you?"

"No. It's a business matter."

"Uh-huh. Well, she doesn't work here any longer. She quit. All of a sudden, not even a single day's notice."

"When was that?"

"Last night, when she closed up. On the phone, for lord's

sake, didn't even have the decency to come and tell me to my face. I couldn't find anybody to replace her on short notice. I shouldn't have opened at all today, I suppose, this rain and all." Then, not so irrelevantly, "I have varicose veins."

"Did she say why she was quitting?"

"Moving away. She didn't say where and I didn't ask."

One more piece to fill out the pattern. "Leaving right away?"

"I suppose so. She didn't tell me that, either." Another breathy sigh. "I'll tell you this: I won't miss her in the long run. She wasn't the best employee I've ever had. Not dishonest, like some, but snotty and snappish to the customers sometimes. Late opening up, too, I had more than one complaint about that. But you take what help you can get these days. I suppose she owes somebody money?"

". . . Money?"

"Why you want to see her. The business matter you spoke of."

I said, "She owes somebody something, that's for sure," and left the woman frowning and running a hand through her hair as if she was petting the black-pelt thing.

14

The rain had slackened into a misty drizzle when I reached the bridge that spans the river near Monte Rio. The wide sandy beach below it on either side was a popular swimming and picnicking spot during the summer months; not much of it was visible now, with the water level up from the recent rains. Once you crossed the bridge, the main road looped to the right into and through the village center, but that was not the way I went. I'd programmed Marie Seldon's address into the GPS, and the disembodied voice I still found vaguely annoying directed me past the turning and onto Old Wood Road, a narrow strip of pitted asphalt that stretched east along the river.

As soon as I made the turn I remembered that I'd been down this road once before, on an exploratory drive with Kerry and Emily one long-ago Sunday, and had forgotten its name. It ran for half a mile or so before dead-ending and was lined with a mixed bag of dwellings, most of them on high grassy banks crowded with pine and rock maple and wild grape that overlooked the river. Rustic cottages large and small, summer homes behind fences and screens of shrubbery, a small, closed

111

resort that had once served food and hosted dances. The area's old-time atmosphere had been palpable enough on a sunny summer day; winter desertion and the gloomy weather created the fanciful impression that I had passed through a time warp into the 1950s.

Marie Seldon's residence was not on the riverfront, but one of a short, staggered row of small cottages at the edge of a pine forest on the inland side. They were all identical in old age, size, and design—resort cottages, probably, that had been turned into rental units. The one that bore her number was partially coated with thick twists of ivy along one side. And it looked as though I'd gotten lucky: a car, an elderly yellow four-door Ford Focus hatchback with the hatch raised, was backed up close in front on an unpaved driveway. If the vehicle was hers, then she was still here.

Right. I had confirmation five seconds after I pulled over onto the grassy verge. The front door opened and out she came, a somewhat chunky blonde in a black windbreaker, toting a large cardboard box.

Her attention was on loading the carton into the back of the Ford; she didn't notice me until I was a third of the way up along the edge of the muddy lane. When she did see me she froze, one hand up on the hatchback lid as if she'd been about to close it. The nearer I got to her, the surer she was that she'd never seen me before and the surer I was that she did not want anything to do with a stranger. Her stance was rigid, her broad mouth set tight, her stare both hostile and wary.

"Who're you? What do you want?"

She flung the words at me when I reached the Ford's nose, but I kept on going to where she stood before I answered. The car's rear seats had been folded down, I saw, and the space behind the front seats was packed with suitcases, cartons, clothing on hangers.

"Marie Seldon?"

"So what if I am?" She had a hard, abrasive voice. Her face was hard, too, pinched, her eyes like flat brown stones—the face of a not very smart woman who had been kicked around and done her share of kicking back. Some men might have found her attractive, in large part because of oversized breasts that bulged the front of the sweater beneath her open windbreaker, but I was not one of them. There was no softness in her, no vulnerability, no indication that she was capable of either compassion or love.

I nodded toward the car. "Moving out?"

"None of your business. What do you want?"

"Some conversation."

"Why? What about? Listen, mister—"

"Ray Fentress," I said.

The name plainly jolted her. "I don't know anybody named Fentress."

"I think you do. I think you met with him in San Francisco last week to discuss something that happened in June of 2014."

"Who the hell are you?" Snapping the words, almost snarling them. "If you're a cop, let me see your ID."

I gave her a close-up look at the photostat of my license. She sneered at it. "Private cop," she said, as if mouthing an obscenity. "Go away; get out of here. I got nothing to say to you."

"Floyd Mears," I said. "Melanie Joy Holloway."

What color there was in Marie's pale face drained away; the rain-damp skin across her cheekbones tightened visibly. But she hung on to her cool; the fact that she was a cold number by nature helped her manage it. "You keep throwing out names of people I never heard of. You better get out of here before I call the real cops, tell 'em you're hassling me with a lot of bullshit I don't know anything about."

"Go ahead, call them."

"You think I won't? Wait around and see."

She slammed the hatchback shut, spun around, and stalked back to the cottage. I had two choices, follow her or leave. If I left, she'd be on the road five minutes after I was gone. I couldn't hang around and then trail her for an extended length of time—only a quarter tank of gas left in my car after the long drive from the city, for one thing—and I did not have enough on her to convince the law to pick her up before she fled the state. I doubted she would carry out her threat to sic sheriff's deputies on me, and I had the idea that if I prodded her a little more she might crack enough to let something incriminating leak through. So I followed her.

She stomped up onto the low porch, yanked the door open. Stopped and half-turned, saw me coming, said something that sounded like, "Bastard!" Then she went in, but she didn't shut the door behind her.

I went up and stood in the open doorway. She was across a small musty living room by then, next to a table that held a brown suede purse. There was a cell phone in her left hand, but she wasn't doing anything with it. The room was mostly empty except for a few sticks of mismatched furniture; she'd finished packing and loading the Ford, and if I had gotten here five minutes later she'd have been gone.

"Go ahead and make the call," I said. "Ask for Lieutenant Heidegger. I'd like to have him in on this."

She neither did nor said anything in response, just glared at me across a dozen feet of empty space.

"You know who Heidegger is, don't you? The man in charge of investigating the double homicide in Floyd Mears' cabin."

"So what?"

"So you were Mears' girlfriend in June of 2014. And Mears and Fentress knew each other from the hunting camp in Lake County. The three of you cooked up and carried out the plan, right?"

"I don't know what the fuck you're talking about." The denial came out sharp, but not as sharp as what she'd said previously. She didn't seem quite so cool any longer.

"Or was it just you and Mears, with Fentress supplying the info on Melanie Holloway? Maybe he didn't even know what the two of you had in mind until it was too late."

Nothing from her.

"How much of the take was he getting? A third? Less than that?"

Still nothing.

"Lot of money in any case," I said. "Six figures altogether."

She put her back to me, lifting the cell phone to her ear. But I didn't see her other hand dive into the purse, didn't see the gun until she whirled around and pointed the damn thing at me.

"All right, you son of a bitch, get your ass in here and shut the door."

I hesitated, tightening up inside, cursing myself for not figuring she might have a firearm close at hand. Age-slowed reflexes, mental as well as physical. The piece was a small automatic, probably a .32, not an optimum weapon for accurate shooting at a distance but deadly enough nonetheless. I could have ducked and run, but I'm not made that way. If I was going to get shot, it would be looking her straight in the eye.

"Do what I told you, goddamn it!"

I stepped inside, swung the door closed with a backhand thrust. Moved forward in short, slow steps—one, two, three before she told me to stop. Eight feet or so separated us then, too far for me to risk rushing her yet. But unless I could talk my way out of this, and there was little enough chance of that, or find a way to create some kind of distraction to give me an edge, I'd have to make the try sooner or later. I kept my eyes on the gun, on her finger curled around the trigger. If the finger tightened . . .

"This isn't going to get you anywhere," I said. "Lieutenant Heidegger knows everything I know."

"Bullshit. Then he'd be here instead of you."

"My partner knows, too. Killing me won't buy you anything."

"Buy some time," she said.

"Not nearly enough. You can't outrun the law, Marie, and you can't hide from it. Be smart: put the gun down; give yourself up."

"Like hell I will." She wiped the back of her free hand over her mouth, smearing her lipstick. Her face glistened with moisture, not all of it from the rain. "How'd you find out what we done?"

"I'm a detective. I get paid to find things out."

Silence for a few beats. Then, "It was Floyd's idea, not mine. I didn't want to do it, kidnapping's a fucking capital crime, but he swore we wasn't gonna hurt the girl and I made sure we didn't. And Jesus, all that money. A quarter of a million dollars . . ."

"What was Fentress' part in it?"

"He told Floyd about the Holloway bitch and then pointed her out. He didn't want any part of the rest of it. Didn't deserve half as much as he was supposed to get, not after he went and got himself arrested and thrown in prison, the stupid bastard. That really screwed things up."

Nervousness was making her talkative. That and the false perception that I knew more than I did. I kept watching the gun, her finger now sliding back and forth across the curve of the trigger.

"How did it screw things up?"

"Floyd, that asshole, he said we couldn't risk spending any of the money right away . . . worried Holloway might call in the FBI. Only supposed to wait for a few months, but then Fentress went all stupid on us. A few months, okay, but not a year and a half or more. I kept saying, 'Let me have my share like we agreed on,' but Floyd wouldn't do it; he said we had to wait until Ray got out."

"To make sure he didn't talk."

"Yeah. Floyd promised him his share'd be waiting. Made me go up to that goddamn prison twice to reassure him. I had to do what he told me even after we had a fight and busted up. He had the money stashed someplace and he wouldn't tell me where."

"Why did you meet Fentress in the city last week?"

"Floyd made me do that, too. Keep him reassured. Let him know when and where we'd make the split."

"At Mears' cabin. Only Fentress wasn't sure he was going to get his cut, so he brought a gun along with him."

Another finger swipe across her mouth. "No," she said. "He never had no gun."

"So you're the one who brought it. And used it."

She was silent again for a little time. The rain was coming down harder now; I could hear it beating on the roof. Then, "It wasn't me killed him and Floyd and the dog."

"No? Then who did?"

Headshake.

I said, "But you were there that night."

"Yeah, I was there, but I swear I didn't know he was gonna kill them. We were just supposed to grab the money and leave 'em tied up. That was the plan, only he . . ."

A kind of wincing tic lifted one corner of her mouth, half-closed the eye above it. She did not like thinking about that night. No, she hadn't committed the killings. Even as hard-boiled as she was, I doubted she was capable of that kind of cold-blooded slaughter; it had a man's stamp on it. Even now, under pressure and despite her threats to shoot me, the way she held the automatic implied she'd have a hard time pulling the trigger.

"Who?" I asked again. "Who's your accomplice?"

Headshake.

"Who, Marie?"

Another sound rose over that of the rain on the roof, the whine and growl of a car coming up the access lane. She cocked her head. "You're about to find out," she said, and in that second her stance shifted slightly and her gaze slid away from me toward the door.

My reaction was pure instinct, without thought or hesitation. I charged her, twisting my body sideways, my chin pulled down against my chest, right arm extended. The unexpectedness of it caught her completely off guard. I was already on her, driving into her with my shoulder, grabbing for the gun when it bucked in her hand with a noise like a baby thunder-clap. The trigger pull was reflexive and without aim; the slug missed me high and by at least a couple of feet.

Force of impact drove her backward, yelling, staggering both of us. I groped a hold on the automatic, tore it out of her grasp in the same instant she went over backward across the flimsy table, her weight collapsing it. She was in the wrong position to break her fall; she hit the floor on her upper back, her head slamming hard off the boards. The cry choked off on impact, became a kind of grunting gurgle.

I'd managed to check my momentum by throwing an arm up just before I collided with the inside wall. But I was still off balance when I heard the door thwack open and the wind come whistling in.

"Marie! What the hell—"

I steadied myself against the wall, swinging my head around. He was standing in the doorway, filling it as I had earlier, and for two or three frozen seconds we stared at each other with a kind of mutual astonishment because he knew me and I knew him.

George Orcutt, the man I'd interviewed at Rio Verdi Propane.

15

I was the first to move. I shoved off the wall, reversing my grip on the automatic's squared barrel so that I could wrap my fingers around the handle. But Orcutt did not want any part of me or the gun. He must have thought I'd shot Marie Seldon, still lying motionless atop the crushed remains of the table; he took one quick look at her, another at me, and then turned tail and bolted.

"Orcutt! Stop or take a bullet!"

It might as well have been a whisper as a shout. Either he didn't believe me or he was caught in the grip of panic; he didn't break stride, just kept running with his head down. The footing on the driveway was bad; his feet slid in the mud, throwing him into a stagger as he lurched around the side of the Ford. I was out through the door by then, into the slashing rain. He was no more than twenty feet ahead of me. A warning shot might have pulled him up short, but I was not about to risk firing out here in the open even though there was nobody else in sight. I had no authority for that kind of action.

I yelled at him again to stop, making another empty threat to fire, and again he ignored me. He lunged between the Ford and his wheels, a four-door black pickup. I cut over so that I was facing toward him as he tried to yank open the driver's door. But the rain had made the handle slick and the ground a quagmire; he slipped and slid again, lost his grip, and nearly fell.

He threw a look in my direction. I made a menacing gesture with the automatic, still advancing, to keep him from another attempt to get into the pickup. His eyes were as big as cocktail onions, his mouth twisted and his vulpine features fear squeezed. Like so many murderers, he was a coward when he was on the other end of a firearm. Once more he neither attacked nor stood his ground but gave in to his panic and fled.

I chased him down to Old Wood Road. The downpour was heavy enough to make the going slow, as if we were both running in that kind of retarded motion you have in dreams, and I had to keep wiping the rain blur out of my eyes to hold him in sight. Orcutt stumbled into the middle of the deserted road, his head swiveling from side to side, then around for another look in my direction. He had nowhere to go, the damned fool, but the panic drove him ahead just the same, at an angle to the left and onto the far verge.

Tall grass and a tangle of blackberry vines separated a pair of homes on the high riverbank, one on a small lot, the other twice as large, with a side yard of pines and shrubbery. Orcutt fought his way around and through the thorn-ridden blackberries—I could see the vines ripping at his coat and pants—and then broke free into the side yard.

I shoved the gun into my coat pocket, panted my way across the road. At first I couldn't see him, but when I moved farther over toward the larger home there he was, clambering down an outside staircase toward the river. The risers were rain slick; toward the bottom he lost his footing and skidded down the last few steps on his ass.

When he was up and running, onto a thin strip of rocky beach, I lost sight of him again. The river, what I could see of it, was a chocolate-brown swirl, its surface pocked with raindrops and spotted with debris. If he tried to cross it, or stumbled and fell into it, he'd drown like the proverbial rat.

The hell with him. No way was I going to chase after him down there. If he didn't end up in the river, he wouldn't get far on foot, wouldn't get far even if he owned or stole another vehicle. I turned back across the road, slogged up the access lane. By the time I reached the black pickup I was soaked to the skin. And wouldn't you know that was when the rain began to let up into nothing more than a light mist.

Orcutt had left his keys in the ignition. I confiscated them. Another Saturday night special and a box of cartridges were stuffed inside the console compartment; I confiscated them, too. Either he was a gun collector or he had a ready source of outlaw weaponry. Hell, maybe both.

There were two suitcases and a duffel bag on the backseat. I left them where they were without touching them, made sure all the doors were locked. A car went past on the road just then, a woman driving and a toddler in the seat beside her; she didn't slow or glance in my direction. When they were out of sight, I turned and reentered the cottage.

Marie Seldon was still lying in a supine sprawl atop the table wreckage, her limbs twitching a little, her eyes open and rolled up with most of the whites showing, a bubble of foamy spit at one corner of her mouth. All the signs of a concussion, possibly a skull fracture.

I did not want to risk moving her, but I couldn't just leave her there like that; I was afraid she might have convulsions, maybe even swallow her tongue. I found a pillow and a blanket in the bedroom, gently eased her over on her side, and propped her head up. Before I covered her I felt the pockets of her windbreaker; her keys were in one of them and I slipped them out. Then I called 911, asked the operator to send an EMT unit.

After that I went outside again to lock the Ford Focus. Where was the money? I wondered. Among all the belongings she'd stuffed into the back? In that duffel bag in Orcutt's pickup? Or had they divvied it up out of lack of complete trust in each other and there was some in each of the vehicles? Right in front of me in any case; they would not have been getting ready to travel without it. I would've liked to search for it, but it was not within the scope of my job to do so. Too bad. I'd never seen a quarter of a million in cash and surely would never have another opportunity.

Back inside, leaving the door open, I checked on Marie Seldon again. Semiconscious now, moaning, still twitching; she was not going to give me any more trouble before the EMT unit arrived. I used a none too clean towel from the bathroom to dry off, hunted up a plastic bag in the kitchen, and deposited the Saturday night special and box of cartridges inside. Then I dragged a chair over in front of the open doorway, where I could sit and watch the yellow car and the pickup and the road beyond, and put in a call to the county sheriff's department in Santa Rosa.

My luck was still holding. This time Lieutenant Heidegger was in.

16

They caught George Orcutt that same night, just outside Ukiah in a stolen car. He tried to outrun the Highway Patrol and ended up in a ditch with minor injuries. He hadn't managed to find himself another firearm and so he'd been taken into custody with a whimper, not a bang.

Marie Seldon suffered a traumatic head injury but no serious damage to what little brain she had. Once she was hospitalized and the initial symptoms treated, she was lucid again—or as lucid as she would ever be.

The two of them fell all over themselves blaming each other for the murders of Ray Fentress and Floyd Mears.

Criminals as a breed are remarkably stupid. Nearly all of them—white-collar, blue-collar, no-collar—fall into the mentally challenged category. The only exceptions are the morally bereft mega-rich, who seem able to misappropriate millions if not billions with casual impunity.

This bunch, to a man and woman, were a classic example. Even though they'd managed initially to pull off a successful caper, it had been doomed to fall apart sooner or later through multiple acts of stupidity. The original crime, kidnapping, and the subsequent one, homicide, are two of the most simple-minded of all felonies; the risk of getting caught is sky-high in both cases and the penalties among the most severe.

Boiled down to essentials, the abduction of Melanie Joy Holloway and its bloody, greed-fueled aftermath happened this way: Ray Fentress, while working on the Holloway estate, overheard the girl talking to a friend about one of her periodic solo gambling trips to the Graton Casino. For some reason he mentioned this in conversation with his new buddy, Floyd Mears, during the last of their joint hunting trips. Later Mears and Marie Seldon commingled half a dozen functioning brain cells and came up with the kidnapping scheme. Fentress was brought into it late. At first he balked at the idea, but the lure of twenty-five thousand dollars for doing nothing more than finding out when Melanie Joy was to make her next solo trip and then pointing her out at the casino was too much for him to resist. The convincer was Mears' assurance that the girl would not be harmed before or after her father ponied up the quarter-mil ransom. Keeping that promise and not spending any of the money were the only smart decisions any of the connivers had made.

From the casino Mears and Seldon followed Melanie to the motel where she was staying, abducted her late-night with their faces masked, took her to Mears' isolated property in the hills, and held her there blindfolded and drugged under Seldon's guard. Vernon Holloway agreed to the ransom demand, believing Mears' telephone threats to kill his daughter if he failed to follow instructions to the letter. After pulling the cash together, he drove to a midnight rendezvous on a back-country road in West Marin and delivered it to a masked

Mears, who subsequently released the girl. Holloway continued to keep everything under wraps, for his own sake as well as that of his severely traumatized daughter, and saw to it she did likewise by orchestrating the dramatic change in her lifestyle.

An attack of conscience during the planning stages of the snatch was the cause of Fentress' heavy drinking. The night of Melanie's abduction was the night he'd had his run-in with the San Francisco cops, his panic reaction the result of too much alcohol after leaving the Graton Casino and fear that the kidnapping scheme had gone awry and his part in it had been discovered. To ensure that he kept his mouth shut, Mears got word to him that the ransom had been paid and the girl released unharmed, and that Fentress' share would be waiting when he'd served his time.

Any of a score of things could have and should have blown up the whole crazy scheme while it was going down. During the eighteen months Fentress was at Mule Creek, too, Mears continuing to risk growing and selling marijuana while sitting on a quarter-of-a-million-dollar stash, for one. Pretty amazing, when you looked at it objectively, that the unraveling hadn't begun until Mears incurred Seldon's hatred by refusing her her share of the ransom and then beating her up.

Being the type of woman who needed a man, she hooked up with Orcutt and then blabbed to him about the kidnapping and the ransom money. Why settle for a half share when they could have it all? Orcutt's idea, so she claimed. So once again half a dozen brain cells conjoined in a witless plan, this one to hijack the $250,000 when the time came for the split.

I believed Seldon's version of what had gone down at Mears' cabin that night. She arranged for Fentress to pick her up in

Monte Rio; that was why he'd written down her address and "7:00 Mon." (He must have later memorized them or I would not have found the paper in his coat pocket). Orcutt, meanwhile, drove up there in his pickup and hid it in the trees near the access lane, guzzling scotch while he waited to nerve up to what lay ahead. When Seldon and Fentress showed, he followed them on foot, armed with the Saturday night special and wearing thin rubber gloves. He circled around through the trees to approach the cabin from the side away from where the dog was chained, then eased up to the front window. A couple of quick looks inside told him when Mears produced the satchel full of ransom money and emptied it onto the table. Then Orcutt had busted in and held Mears and Fentress at gunpoint.

Seldon knew where Mears kept his .45; she fetched it, turned it over to Orcutt, then gathered up the money. Her story was that Orcutt ordered her to wait outside; more likely she'd made a quick exit on her own so she wouldn't have to watch the wet work. Orcutt claimed Mears tried to jump him and he acted in self-defense, but I figured that was bullcrap. He shot Mears in cold blood with the Saturday night special, switched guns or fired the automatic left-handed and killed a terrified Fentress. Then he went outside and blew away the Doberman so he could get inside the shed.

In the cabin again, he created the rest of the illusion of a marijuana deal gone bad. He planted some of the dope on Fentress, put the Saturday night special into Fentress' dead hand and his own hand over it, and fired a few wild shots. And did the same with Mears and the .45. Pretty weak stage setting, all things considered, but it had held up because there seemed to be no other plausible reason for the carnage.

Afterward Seldon and Orcutt went to his apartment, where according to her he finished off the bottle of scotch. That explained his nervous hangover when I interviewed him at Rio Verdi Propane the next day.

As for the ransom money, Seldon and Orcutt had in fact split it up that night, even though their plan was to run off together. Half of it turned up in her Ford, the other half in the duffel bag in his pickup. There was not much doubt in my mind that if they'd managed to get away with the cash, some dark night one of them would have ended up dead and the entire boodle in the greedy clutches of the other.

Some pack of pea-brained thieves and murderers. Some towering monument to stupidity.

You'd think Vernon Holloway would have been happy that his daughter's kidnappers were identified and punished and to have the entire $250,000 returned to him. But from all indications he wasn't. He continued to make a concerted effort to keep the lid screwed down tight on the abduction, but of course it leaked out anyway. There was something of a media swarm, during which I was outed as the principal catalyst, so Holloway was well aware of the extent of my involvement. I neither expected nor received an expression of gratitude from him; I never heard from him at all, or from anybody connected with him.

The silence was welcome. The less contact I have with the one-percenters, the better.

The hardest thing I had to do was tell Doreen Fentress the truth about her husband, why and how he'd died. She took it better than I'd expected, dry-eyed despite the obvious pain it gave her; if she had any tears left, she would shed them in private.

"It's terrible, what Ray did," she said, "but even so he wasn't a bad man. Just easily led. And he wanted that farm so much."

Excuses, I thought. But I didn't say so.

"At least now I know he wasn't a murderer. That's something to be grateful for."

I supposed it was. He hadn't left her anything else to be grateful for, had he?

GRAPPLIN'

He was sitting on one of the anteroom chairs when I came into the agency that morning. A rather shabbily dressed black man well up in his seventies, thin and on the frail side, with a mostly hairless, liver-spotted scalp, rheumy eyes, a long ridged upper lip, and the kind of slumped posture and pain-etched features that indicate failing health. At first glance you might have taken him for one of San Francisco's legion of homeless street people, but only at first glance. His jacket and slacks were frayed and threadbare, but clean, he wore a tie over a patterned shirt, and his seamed cheeks looked freshly shaven. On his lap were an old brown hat with a faded red band that might once have had a feather stuck in it, and a battered case the size and shape of a trumpet. I had never seen him before.

The door to Tamara's office was open and I could hear her rattling around in the back alcove where we kept a hot plate. Getting coffee for herself and the visitor, I thought.

"Morning," I said to him.

"Mornin'." His voice had traces of a southern accent and was stronger than the rest of him looked, with a gravelly quality that made me think of Louis Armstrong. "You Miz Corbin's partner?"

"That's me." I added my name to confirm it.

He said his name was Charles Anthony Brown, and we shook hands. His palm was so dry it had the feel of fine-grain sandpaper. "Heard of you," he said, then, "what you and Miz Corbin willin' to do for poor folks. That's why I come here. Times, they sure do change."

I didn't need to ask him what he meant by the first and last statements. The first referred to the advertised fact that we took on pro bono cases now and then, mainly for minorities who otherwise couldn't afford detective services—an estimable idea of Tamara's when the agency began to prosper under her direction. The second referred to our partnership—computer-savvy, street-savvy black woman in her late twenties, old-school white guy with forty-plus of his sixty-five years in law enforcement and detective work. It was the kind of alliance that would not have been possible back when Charles Anthony Brown was young, particularly if he was originally from south of the Mason-Dixon line.

There were footsteps and Tamara appeared in the doorway. "I thought I heard your voice," she said to me.

"Just getting acquainted with Mr. Brown."

"He'd like us to locate his niece for him."

"Robin Louise," Brown said, nodding.

Tamara smiled at him. "Coffee's ready in my office. Be more comfortable talking in there."

He nodded and got up slowly, the hat in one hand and the trumpet case in the other. Tamara's glance in my direction was an invitation to join the interview. Brown followed her into the office, moving in a shuffling gait that had everything to do with age and infirmity and nothing to do with the old racial stereotype, and I followed him. She indicated the client's chair nearest her desk, the one within easy reach of the steaming coffee mug she'd set there.

"Milk and three teaspoons of sugar, right?"

"Always did like it sweet," Brown said.

While he was lowering himself into the chair, I went into the alcove and poured myself some coffee and then came back and sat down in the client chair's mate. Tamara was tapping away on her computer keyboard, getting a casefile started. Brown sipped from his mug with one hand; the other continued to grip the trumpet case.

He saw me looking at the case. "My horn," he said. "Never go anywheres without it."

"Are you a professional musician?" I asked.

"Most of my life." He tugged at his ridged upper lip as if offering proof; then his mouth stretched in a small, mirthless smile that revealed missing and neglected teeth. "Too old and broke-down to play in a band. Outdoors now, when the weather's good."

Street musician. There are a lot of them, men and some women of all ages, spotted around the city: Embarcadero Center Plaza, Pier 39, Ghirardelli Square, Civic Center, the entrances to BART stations, on random corners—anywhere there is heavy foot traffic and the likelihood of somebody willing to part with dollar bills or coins for a few minutes' entertainment. It may be a form of panhandling, but it's considerably more honest than the direct, too often aggressive solicitation. Those who possess a reasonable degree of talent can make enough to get by, if they don't spend it all on alcohol or drugs. Brown didn't seem to have any of the telltale signs of either addiction.

"But I don't sleep outdoors," he said. "I ain't homeless. Got me a room and a job cleanin' up at the Blue Moon Café on Howard Street. Got a little money saved up to give my niece when you find her."

"There's no need to explain—"

"Just wanted you to know."

Tamara said, "What's your niece's full name, Mr. Brown?"

"Robin Louise"—slight pause—"Arceneaux."

"How do you spell the last name?"

He spelled it for Tamara and she typed it into the computer file.

"When did you last have any contact with her?"

"Long time ago. Way too long."

"How long, approximately?"

"Fifty-one years," he said. "Summer, 1963."

Tamara and I exchanged glances.

"How old was your niece at that time?" I asked him.

"Seven years old. Born in '56, April 18."

"Have you had any contact with her since then? Phone conversations, letters?"

"No."

"Tried to locate her before now?"

"No."

"Mind if we ask why?"

Brown didn't care for the question; it showed in his rheumy eyes. But he said, "Just lost touch, that's all. Lot of reasons. Travelin' around the country, workin', playin' my music."

"You realize she might not still be living?"

He didn't like that one, either. A muscle jumped in his cheek. "She's alive," he said emphatically. "Got to be."

Tamara asked, "Who was she living with in 1963? Father, mother, both?"

He sat for a few seconds without answering. Then his face suddenly bunched up and he was seized by a fit of coughing. He fumbled a handkerchief out of his pocket to cover his mouth until the spell passed. It left him wheezing and with a sickly gray undertone to his dark features.

Tamara asked if he was all right. He said, "For the time bein'. Comes and goes. What'd you ask me before?"

"If your niece was living with her father, mother, or both in 1963."

"With her mama's sister Jolene and her man. Jolene and Bobby Franklin."

Tamara's computer keys clicked again. "Where was this?"

"N'Orleans."

"The city itself or a suburb?"

"French Quarter. Dauphine Street."

"Do you remember the number?"

Headshake. "My memory ain't so good anymore."

"What about the girl's parents? Something happen to them?"

"They both died."

"How and when?"

Another headshake. He didn't seem to want to answer the question.

"Last name Arceneaux. What were their given names?"

Or that one. It took him three or four seconds to say, "Don't matter. Robin Louise, she with Jolene and Bobby Franklin like I said. They raised her up."

"All right. What did the Franklins do for a living?"

"Jolene worked in one of the clubs, don't remember which. Bobby, he was a drummer. Good one, too. Real good chops."

"Play with a particular band?"

"Don't remember." Brown seemed agitated now. "Listen, ain't I already told you enough so you can find Robin Louise?"

"The more information we have—"

A second bout of coughing struck him, not as intense as the first. He covered his mouth with the handkerchief again, and this time I could see flecks of blood on the fabric.

When the fit passed and he had his breath back, he said, "Already told you all I remember. Find her from that, can't you?"

"I think so. Do our best."

"Got to be soon," he said. "I ain't got much time left. You can see the kind of shape I'm in."

"Are you under a doctor's care?" I asked.

"Can't afford no doctor."

"There are free clinics—"

"Charity. No, sir. Wouldn't do no good anyway. Man gets to be my age, he knows when his time's near up. Be playin' a duet with Gabriel pretty soon now." The wry little mouth stretch again. "Or maybe Old Scratch, if I end up down below."

What can you say to that? Tamara and I were both silent.

Brown finished his coffee. "I got to be goin' now," he said, and used the corner of the desk to shove up onto his feet.

I walked out with him. On the way he stumbled once and I caught hold of his arm, but he shrugged my hand off more or less gently. Didn't want to be helped. Pride.

At the door he clamped the battered old hat on his head. "Don't know where I'll be rest of today," he said then. "But tonight, any night after six o'clock, I'll be at the Blue Moon Café. All right?" He waited for my nod, and then he was gone.

• • •

Tamara had other, pressing business to attend to and had only just started on the Robin Louise Arceneaux trace when I left for the day. Now that I'm semiretired, my time at the agency is generally limited to two nonconsecutive days a week. But I had some leftover work on an insurance fraud case to finish up, so I went in again the following morning.

My partner is a workaholic and as usual she was already at her computer. What wasn't usual this morning was that she was humming as she worked, something I had never heard her do before. The tune had an old-fashioned bluesy rhythm. Jazz is my favorite type of music and I'm fairly knowledgeable, but this was one I didn't recognize.

"What's that you're humming?"

She hadn't heard me come in, hadn't realized I was standing behind her. She broke off and swung around in her chair to look up at me. There are several different mood-driven personas occupying her plump young body, most but not all of them pleasant; you're never sure quite which one you're going to face on a given day. The one I was looking at this morning was Glum Tamara. Curious. As bluesy as the tune had been, it had also had a lively beat that didn't fit with the Glum Tamara persona.

"Old jazz song," she said.

"I gathered as much. What's it called?"

" 'Who You Been Grapplin' With?' "

"Catchy title."

"Yeah."

"I don't think I've heard it before. Sounds Dixieland."

"It is. New Orleans club band called the Sweetmeat Five cut a record of it in '59, but it didn't get much play until the early sixties, after . . ." She let the rest of the sentence trail off and said instead, "Pretty much been forgotten since."

"Where'd you come across it?"

"Internet," she said. "And a dude I know collects old jazz records."

She surprised me again, then—twice. First by closing her eyes and starting to sing softly, something else she'd never before done in my presence, and second by the low, smoky, Billie Holiday quality of her voice.

"Who you been grapplin' with, ba-by?
While I been away.
Who you been grapplin' with, hon-ey?
Every night and day.

"Who you gonna grapple with, ba-by?
Now I'm home to stay.
Who you gonna grapple with, hon-ey?
Every night and day.

"Well, I'll tell you, sweet dad-dy,
The way it's gonna be.
Yeah, I'll tell you, sweet dad-dy,
You better grapple with me.
Every night and day—nobody but me."

Tamara let out a long sighing breath. "There're more verses, but those are the only three I remember."

"I didn't know you could sing."

"Yeah, well, mostly in the shower."

"You ought to do it more often—you have a nice voice."

The compliment didn't seem to cheer her much. Her smile was fleeting. "Wish I could get the damn song out of my head."

"Why? It has a good beat."

"You think so? Bet the man who wrote it doesn't anymore."

"No? Who would he be?"

"Moses Arceneaux."

"Arceneaux. Related to Charles Brown's niece?"

"Robin Louise isn't his niece, she's his daughter. Charles Anthony Brown's real name is Moses Arceneaux."

"Oh," I said, "so that's it."

"That's it."

"So why did he lie to us? Why the false name?"

"Man's a fugitive, that's why," Tamara said. "Been a fugitive ever since 1963."

Well, that explained her glumness. "What's he wanted for?"

"Double homicide. Murdered his wife and her lover, another musician named Dupres."

She handed me a couple of pages of printout. Her computer skills are exceptional; if there is information on any topic available anywhere online, she'll find it. What she'd pulled up here were a copy of the fugitive warrant issued by the New Orleans police department in August of 1963 and a brief newspaper account of the crimes. The gist of both was that Moses Arceneaux, jazz trumpeter, songwriter, and member of the Sweetmeat Five, had in cold blood and with malice aforethought shot to death his wife, Lily, the band's lead singer, and a jazz pianist with another group named Marcus Dupres. He'd done this, it was alleged, in a jealous rage after finding out that the two were having an affair. Two neighbors of Dupres who'd heard the shots had arrived on the scene in time to witness Arceneaux standing over his wife's body with the murder

weapon, a .38 revolver registered to him, in his hand. Arceneaux had immediately dropped the weapon and taken flight.
After which he had evidently stopped at his own apartment
long enough to gather some cash and a few personal belongings, then fled the city and disappeared without a trace.

The fact that he had continued to evade capture for more
than half a century was not as amazing as it might seem. There
were other such cases on record—men and women who had
changed their identities, maintained a low profile, and done
nothing to attract police attention and either were never caught
during their lifetimes or for one reason or another were finally
found and brought to justice. Still, half a century is a lot of
years to be on the run. Moses Arceneaux had beaten long odds.
Very long odds.

"Damn," I said when I returned the printout. "I liked that
man."

"So did I. So what do we do now?"

"You know the answer to that. What we're bound to do by
law—turn him in. There's no statute of limitations on homicide."

"Even though he's old and sick?"

"The two people he shot never had a chance to grow old."

"Yeah. But maybe they had it coming to them."

"Nobody has murder coming to them."

Tamara knew that as well as I did; she didn't put up any
more argument. "But not with a phone call, okay? He came to
us on his own, he's a client no matter what he did fifty years
ago, and he's dying . . . can't treat the man cold that way."

"No, we can't and we won't. I'll take him in."

"Right away?"

"Tonight," I said. "I don't want to have to go looking for
him on the streets, make a public thing out of it."

"I could go along—"

"What for? Wouldn't make it any easier."

". . . I guess not."

"What about Robin Louise?" I asked. "You locate her?"

"No problem with that. She was raised by Jolene and Bobby Franklin, all right—the murdered wife's sister and her husband. They adopted her, had her last name legally changed to Franklin."

"Is she still living?"

"In Shreveport. Trained and working now as a physical therapist. Married once to a man named Davis. Two children, both grown. Old Moses doesn't even know he's a grandpop." Tamara's mouth took on a lemony twist. "Sometimes I hate this damn business."

"Yeah," I said. "So do I."

The Blue Moon Café was on the fringe of Skid Row, in that section below Market Street that used to be called South of the Slot. Much of the old warehouse district farther south had undergone urban renewal, was now home to nightclubs and expensive condos and loft apartments and known locally as SoMa. But the Skid Row pocket remained mostly unchanged, as filled as ever with drunks and drug addicts and hookers and scruffy bars and cheap lodging places, like an ugly piece of the city caught in a time warp. You walked carefully in that neighborhood after dark. I walked carefully even though it was only seven o'clock and just dusk when I got there.

The café was not quite a greasy spoon, though grease was one of the dominant odors along with beer and human effluvium. One long, wide room with a counter along the right-hand wall, booths along another, and several tables in two rows down the middle. The kitchen was at the rear and wrapped partway around behind the counter. An open corridor yawned on its other side.

Business was good at this hour: more than half of the spaces were occupied by a mixed-race and mostly poverty-level clientele. There was the low buzz of conversation, but none of the punctuations of laughter you heard in better restaurants. Eating was serious business here. And not a particularly enjoyable one, judging from the samples of the fare I saw in passing and the expressions worn by the diners.

I found an open spot at the counter, and when a tired-looking Latina waitress got around to me I said I was there to see Charles Anthony Brown. Her expression of surprise indicated he had few if any callers, but she didn't ask questions. "Down past the johns," she said, gesturing. "Last door on the left."

Kitchen and bathroom smells were strong in the dimly lit corridor. The two doors on the left were unmarked. I stopped at the last one, knocked, and pretty soon it opened and he peered out at me. Recognition put a look of hope in the rheumy eyes—and I took it away quick because there was no other, more merciful way to do it.

"Hello, Moses," I said.

He stood frozen for half a dozen beats. Other emotions flickered briefly in his eyes and on his deeply seamed face; the one that remained, I thought, was resignation.

"So you found out," he said.

"Did you really believe we wouldn't?"

"Figured you might. It don't matter much anymore. You gonna take me to the po-lice now?"

"Let's talk a little first."

He backed up slowly into the room. I stepped inside, closed

the door against the dish rattle and voice murmurs out front. The room was a windowless, fourteen-by-fourteen box, dimly lit by a low-wattage ceiling bulb, that had once been used for storage; still was, to an extent, judging by the cartons stacked along one wall. In the remaining space were a cot covered with an old army blanket, a rickety chair, a small table, and a kind of open, makeshift closet that contained Moses Arceneaux's meager belongings. I wondered if he realized how much the room looked and felt like what he'd spent fifty-one years avoiding—a prison cell.

His trumpet lay on the cot. He caught it up when he sat down, held it on his lap. It was old and a little dinged here and there, but the brass surfaces still shone from myriad polishings. The one thing he owned that he cared about, I thought.

He said, "You find Robin Louise?"

"Yes, we found her. She lives in Shreveport."

"Knew she was still alive. Knew it for sure."

"She may not want to have anything to do with you," I said. "You must know that, too."

"I believe she will. Got some money saved for her, like I told you yesterday. Got to talk to her one last time before I die. Tell her I'm sorry. Tell her I never stopped loving her. Tell her the truth."

"What truth?"

"About what happened to her mama and Marcus Dupres that night in '63." Arceneaux ran his long, gnarled fingers around the rim of the trumpet's bell. "Tell you the truth, too, you want to hear it."

"Go ahead."

"I didn't kill Lily or that piano man," he said, "neither of 'em."

I said nothing. The number of men and women charged with capital crimes who profess their innocence to the bitter end are countless. Nearly all such claims are self-serving obfuscations or outright lies. Ninety-five percent, at a reasonable guess. But it's the five percent that make a cry of innocence worth listening to.

"Swear it on a Bible," Arceneaux said. "I never done it."

I stayed mute.

He put the wrong interpretation on my silence. "You like everybody down in N'Orleans," he said, "you don't believe it." Surprisingly, there was no discernible bitterness in the words.

"Suppose you tell me the way it was."

"I loved that woman, that's the way it was. Even after I found out she was cheatin' on me with that piano man. I might've whipped her ass some if I'd had the chance, but kill her dead? No, sir. Never."

"She was shot with your pistol. Both of them were."

"Not by me. Didn't happen the way it looked."

"All right. How did it happen?"

"Kind of hard to remember exactly, after so many years." A bunch of seconds went by while he either worked his memory or built a framework of lies.

Then he said, "Horn man in Dupres' band told me about her and him. Drunk, and he let it slip out. Man, it cut me deep. I was half outa my head, I admit that, when I went harin' over to Dupres' place that night."

"With your pistol in your pocket."

"No, sir. Lily was the one brought the gun. Dupres been stringin' her along, told her they was gonna run off together. She believed him, must've wanted him bad, more'n she ever wanted me, but then she found out he had him another woman besides her, stringin' that one along, too. She had a bad temper,

Lily did. Didn't go to Dupres' place for screwin' that night, went there for a showdown—make him choose between her and his other woman. That's why she took the pistol with her."

"How do you know all this?"

"They was yellin' it at each other when I got there," Arceneaux said. "Bastard must've hit her 'cause I heard a sound like a slap, and she screamed, and next thing I heard was that gun goin' off. Door wasn't locked. I got it open and run inside, and Dupres was on the floor with blood all over his face and Lily standin' there with her eyes crazy wild. She swung around on me wavin' the pistol like she was gonna shoot me, too. I tried to take it away from her, we grappled some, and . . . Lord, it went off again and she fell down dead as Dupres. Somebody come runnin' in then, must've been one of the neighbors, and somebody else outside was hollerin' for the cops, and there I was holdin' the pistol that killed 'em both. . . ."

"So you panicked and ran."

"Yeah, that's what I done. I threw the gun down and hauled ass outa there. I didn't have no other choice."

"Sure you did. You could've stayed and told the police what you just told me."

He laughed, a hollow sound that morphed suddenly into one of his coughing fits. It took a little while, once the spell subsided, before he was able to go on talking.

"Man, you don't know what it was like down south in them Jim Crow days. Black man in a room with his dead wife and her dead lover and his own pistol smokin' in his hand. You think they'd of believed me? No way. They'd of thrown me in jail, likely beat on me, then put me in prison and the 'lectric chair. I wouldn't of stood a chance in hell. Sure, I ran. Ain't been closer to N'Orleans than five hundred miles since."

"Fifty years of running and hiding," I said. "What'd you do all that time?"

"Stayed out of trouble. Swear that on a Bible, too—I ain't never once broke the law, nor even been tempted to. Mr. Good Citizen everywhere I went, one end of the country to the other. Never stayed too long in one place until I come out here to San Fran, been here seven years now. Worked to put food in my belly and clothes on my back, any kind of job I could get where I didn't have to show identification. Pickin' crops. Washin' dishes. Diggin' ditches. Janitor work, handyman work." He ran his hands over the trumpet again, fingered the buttons. "Played and sang on the streets. In backstreet bars now and then, when I could get a gig and I was sure wouldn't nobody recognize me or my style. Guess I been lucky."

Yeah, I thought. Lucky.

I said, "And you have no regrets?"

"About runnin' off the way I done? No. My music . . . yeah, some there, but the band I played with in N'Orleans wasn't goin' nowhere and neither was I. Only wrote one song that was any good, 'Who You Been Grapplin' With?' Leavin' and losin' my daughter, that's my only regret. But I knew she'd be all right, I knew her auntie'd take care of her."

"You could have at least tried to find out."

"Did once, year or so after. Man I knew, only one I figured I could trust, I got in touch with him and he told me Jolene and Bobby was gonna adopt Robin Louise. I asked him to keep an eye on her and he said he would, but he went and got himself killed in an accident."

"And you never tried to contact her until now?"

"Thought about it plenty. Come close a dozen times, but I never could nerve myself up to it. Too scared of the po-lice, dyin' in prison for something I never done. Never stopped bein' scared until just a little while ago, when I come to know for sure my time was almost up. Funny thing. Now I ain't scared anymore."

I had been watching him closely as he laid out his story. When you've been lied to as often as I have over the years, by all sorts of people good and bad, you develop ways to separate the truths from the untruths, a kind of homespun lie detector. Body language: nervous gestures, facial tics, shifty looks, or too-direct eye contact. Statements too glib or overly earnest, points glossed over or omitted or contradictory, voice inflections that don't ring true. I'd neither seen nor heard any of those telltale indicators in Moses Arceneaux or his account of what had happened that August night in 1963.

He'd told me the truth, the whole truth. I would have staked my reputation on it.

The man was not a murderer, not a criminal. Just the opposite, in fact—a victim of circumstance, and racial prejudice, and the kind of crippling fear that overrides all other human emotions.

He sat slumped now, as if the conversation had exhausted him. His dark face was beaded with sweat; that and the glow from the pale ceiling bulb gave it an oddly burnished quality, like a casting in bronze.

"We goin' to the po-lice now?" he said.

I'd already made up my mind. Sometimes you have to go with your gut instincts and to hell with rules and regulations and strict adherence to the letter of the law. There is more than one kind of justice in this world, even if it's too little and too late.

"No," I said. "No reason to, Mr. Brown."

". . . Brown?"

"Our client is Charles Anthony Brown. As far as we know, nobody by that name is wanted by the authorities."

I handed him Tamara's printout containing the personal and contact information for Robin Louise Franklin Davis. He looked at it, looked up at me with emotions playing over his face again—gratitude, renewed hope, something that might have been shame.

"Good-bye, Mr. Brown," I said. "Good luck with Robin Louise."

I went to the door. I had my hand on the knob when the trumpet notes sounded behind me, tentative at first, then clear and sharp and now familiar. When I turned back toward him, he lowered the instrument and said, "I ain't played nor sung 'Who You Been Grapplin' With?' in fifty years, 'cept inside my head. Lily's song, wrote it special for her, but it's mine now. Been mine ever since I left N'Orleans."

I didn't say anything. There was nothing left to say.

In a low, age-cracked voice, he began to sing. The melody was the same, but the beat was slower, the lyrics slightly different and with different meaning than the ones Tamara had sung for me—a mournful elegy for a tragically broken life that stayed with me long after I left him.

> *"Who you been grapplin' with, Mo-ses?*
> *Since back in '63.*
> *Who you been grapplin' with, Mo-ses?*
> *I been grapplin' with me.*
> *Lord, Lord, I been grapplin' with me."*

NIGHTSCAPE

Jake Runyon and I were the only customers in the all-night diner near the Cow Palace, sitting at the counter with mugs of coffee for me and tea for him, when the man and woman blew in out of the rain.

Blew in is the right phrase. They came fast through the door, leaning forward, prodded by the howling wind. Nasty night out there. One of the hard-rain, big-wind storms that hammer the California coast during an El Niño winter.

The man shook himself doglike, shedding rainwater off a shaved head and a threadbare topcoat, before the two of them slid into one of the sidewall booths. That was as much attention as I paid to them at first. He wasn't the man we were waiting for.

"After eleven," I said to Runyon. "Looks like Maxwell's a no-show again tonight."

"Weather like this, he'll probably stay holed up."

"And so we get to do it all over again tomorrow night."

"You want to give it a few more minutes?"

"Might as well. At least until the rain lets up a little."

Floyd Maxwell was a deadbeat dad, the worst kind. Spousal

abuser who owed his ex more than thirty thousand dollars in unpaid child support for their two kids; hard to catch because he kept moving around in and out of the city, never staying in one place longer than a couple of months, and because he had the kind of job—small-business computer consultant—that allowed him to work from any location. Our agency had been hired by the ex's father and we'd tracked Maxwell to this neighborhood, but we'd been unable to pinpoint an exact address; all we knew was that since he'd moved here he ate in the Twenty-Four Seven Diner most evenings after ten o'clock, when there were few customers. Bracing him was a two-man job because of his size and his history of violent behavior. Runyon was twenty years younger than me, and had a working knowledge of judo learned during his days as a Seattle cop.

This was our third night staked out here and so far all we had to show for it were sour stomachs from too much caffeine. I had mixed feelings about the job anyway. On the one hand I despise deadbeat dads and spousal abusers and nailing one is always a source of satisfaction. On the other hand it amounted to a bounty hunt, the two of us sitting here with handcuffs in our pockets waiting to make a citizens' arrest of a fugitive, and I've never much cared for that kind of strong-arm work. Or the type of people who do it for a living.

The new couple were the only other customers right now. The counterman, a thin young guy with a long neck and not much chin, leaned over the counter and called out to them, "What can I get you folks?"

"Coffee," the man said. He was about forty, well set up, pasty-faced and hard-eyed. Some kind of tattoo crawled up the side of his neck; another covered the back of one hand. He glanced at the woman. "You want anything to eat, Lila?"

"No."

"Couple of hamburgers to go," he said to the counterman. "One with everything, one with just the meat. Side of fries."

"Anything to drink?"

"More coffee, biggest carton you got. Milk."

"For the coffee?"

"In another carton. For drinking."

The counterman said, "Coming up," and turned to the grill.

The tattooed guy said to the woman, "You better have something. We got a long drive ahead of us."

"I couldn't eat, Kyle." She was maybe thirty, a washed-out, purse-lipped blonde who might have been pretty once—the type of woman who perpetually makes the wrong choices with the wrong people and shows the effects. "I feel kind of sick."

"Yeah? Why didn't you stay in the car?"

"You know why. I couldn't listen to it anymore."

"Well, you better get used to it."

"It breaks my heart. I still think—"

"I don't care what you think. Just shut up."

Lila subsided, slouching down in the booth so that her head rested against the low back. Runyon and I were both watching them now, without being obvious about it. Eye-corner studies with our heads held still.

Pretty soon the woman said, "Why'd we have to stop here, so close? Why couldn't we keep going?"

"It's a lousy night and I'm hungry, that's why."

"Hungry. After what just happened I don't see how you—"

"Didn't I just tell you to shut up?"

The counterman set a mug of steaming coffee on the counter. "You'll have to come get it," he said. "I got to watch the burgers."

Neither of the pair made a move to leave the booth. Kyle leaned forward and snapped at her in a low voice, "Well? Don't just sit there like a dummy. Get the coffee."

Grimacing, she slid out and fetched the coffee for him. She didn't sit down again. "I don't feel so good," she said.

"So go outside, get some air."

"No. I think I'm gonna be sick."

"Yeah, well, don't do it here, for Christ sake."

She turned away from him, putting a hand up to cover her mouth, and half-ran into the areaway that led to the restrooms. A door slammed back there. Kyle loaded sugar into his coffee, made slurping sounds as he drank.

"Hurry up with the food," he called to the counterman.

"Almost ready."

It got quiet in there, except for the meat-sizzle on the grill, the French fries cooking in their basket of hot oil. Outside, the wind continued to beat at the front of the diner, but the rain seemed to have slacked off some.

Runyon and I watched Kyle finish his coffee. For a few seconds he sat drumming on the tabletop. Then he smacked it with his palm, slid out, and came up to the counter two stools down from where we were sitting. He stood watching the counterman wrap the burgers in waxed paper, put them into a sack with the fries; pour coffee into one container, milk into another.

"How much?" he said.

"Just a second while I ring it up."

Kyle looked over toward the areaway, scowling. Lila still hadn't reappeared.

"Hope your friend's okay," the counterman said.

"Mind your own business, pal."

The total for the food and drinks was fourteen dollars. Kyle dragged a worn wallet out of his pocket, slapped three bills down next to the two bags. When he did that I had a clear look at the tattoo on his hand—Odin's Cross. There were bloody scrapes across the knuckles on that hand, crimson spots on the sleeve of his topcoat; the blood hadn't completely coagulated yet. Under the open coat, on the left side at the belt, I had a glimpse of wood and metal.

I was closest to him and he caught me paying attention. "What the hell you looking at?"

I didn't say anything.

"Keep your eyes to yourself, man, you know what's good for you."

I let that pass, too.

Lila came back from the restroom looking pale. "About the damn time," Kyle said to her.

"I couldn't help it. I told you I was sick."

"Take those sacks and let's go."

She picked up the sacks and they started for the door. As far as Lila was concerned, the rest of us weren't even there; she was focused on Kyle and her own misery. Otherwise she might have been more careful about what she said on the way.

"Kyle . . . you won't hurt him, will you?"

"Don't be stupid."

"You hit him twice already. . . ."

"A couple of slaps, big deal. He's not hurt."

"You get crazy sometimes. What you did to his mother—"

"Goddammit, keep your voice down."

"But what if she calls the—"

"She won't. She knows better. Now shut up!"

They were at the door by then. And out into the gibbering night.

I glanced at Runyon. "Who's the plain burger and milk for, if she's too sick to eat?"

"Yeah," he said, and we were both off our stools and moving. Trust your instincts.

At the door I said, "Watch yourself. He's armed."

"I know. I saw it, too."

Outside the rain had eased up to a fine drizzle, but the wind was still beating the night in bone-chilling gusts. The slick black street and sidewalks were empty except for the man and the woman off to our right, their backs to us, Kyle moving around to the driver's door of a Subaru Outback parked two car lengths away. There was a beeping sound as he used the remote on his key chain to unlock the doors.

Runyon and I made our approach in long silent strides, not too fast. You don't want to call attention to yourself by running or making noise in a situation like this; it only invites a panic reaction. What we did once Kyle saw us depended on what he did. The one thing we wouldn't do was to give chase if he jumped into the car, locked the doors, and drove away; that kind of macho nonsense is strictly Hollywood. In that scenario we'd back off and call 911 and let the police handle it.

The woman, Lila, opened the passenger side door. The dome light came on, providing a vague lumpish view of a rear cargo space packed with suitcases and the like. But it was what spilled out from the backseat, identifiable in the wind-lull that followed, that tightened muscles all through my body. A child crying in broken, frightened sobs.

We were nearing the Outback by then, off the curb and into the street. Close enough to make out the rain-spattered license plate. 5QQX700—an easy one to remember. But I didn't need to remember it. The way things went down, the plate number was irrelevant.

Lila saw us first. She called, "Kyle!" and jerked back from the open passenger door.

He was just opening the driver's side. He came around fast, but he didn't do anything else for a handful of seconds. Just stood there staring at us as we advanced, still at the measured pace, Runyon a couple of steps to my left so we both had a clear path at him.

Runyon put up a hand, making it look nonthreatening, and said in neutral tones, "Talk to you for a minute?"

No. It wasn't going to go down that way—reasonable, nonviolent.

At that moment a car swung around the corner up ahead, throwing mist-smeared headlight glare over the four of us and the Outback. The light seemed to jump-start Kyle. He didn't try to get inside; he jammed the door shut and went for the weapon he had under his coat.

Runyon got to him first, just as the gun came out, and knocked his arm back.

A beat or two later I shouldered into him, hard, pinning the left side of his body against the wet metal. That gave Runyon time to judo-chop his wrist, a blow that loosed his grip on the gun. A second chop drove it right out of his hand, sent it clattering along the pavement.

Things got a little wild then. Kyle fought us, snarling; he was big and angry and even though there were two of us, just as big, he was no easy handful. The woman stood off from the Outback, yelling like a banshee. The other car, the one with the lights, skidded to a stop across the street. The wind howled;

the child shrieked. I had a vague aural impression of running footsteps, someone else yelling.

It took maybe a minute's worth of teamwork to put an end to the struggle. I managed finally to get a two-handed hold on Kyle's arms, which allowed Runyon to step free and slam the edge of his hand down on the exposed joining of neck and shoulder. The blow paralyzed the right side of Kyle's body. After that we were able to wrestle him to the wet pavement, stretch him out belly down. I yanked his arms back, held them while Runyon knelt in the middle of his spine and snapped handcuffs around his wrists.

I stood up first, breathing hard—and a white, scared face was peering at me through the rear side window. A little boy, six or seven, wrapped in a blanket, his cheeks streaked with tears. Past him, on the other side of the car, I could see Lila standing, quiet now, with both hands fisted against her mouth.

Runyon said, "Where's the gun?"

"I don't know. I heard it hit the pavement—"

"I've got it."

I turned around. It was the guy from the car that had pulled up across the street; he'd come running over to rubberneck. He stood a short distance away, holding the revolver in one hand, loosely, as if he didn't know what to do with it. Heavyset and bald, I saw as I went up to him. Eyebrows like miniature tumbleweeds.

"What's going on?" he said.

"Police business."

"Yeah? You guys cops?"

"Making an arrest." I held out my hand, palm up. "Let's have the gun."

He hesitated, but only briefly. "Sure, sure," he said then, and laid it on my palm.

And I backed up a step and pointed it at a spot two inches below his chin.

"Hey!" He gawped at me in disbelief. "Hey, what's the idea?"

"The idea," I said, "is for you to turn around, slow, and clasp your hands together behind you. Do it—now!"

He did it. He didn't have any choice.

I gave the piece to Runyon. And then, shaking my head, smiling a little, I snapped my set of handcuffs around Floyd Maxwell's wrists.

Funny business, detective work. Crazy business sometimes. Mostly it's a lot of dull routine, with small triumphs and as much frustration as satisfaction. But once in a great while something happens that not only makes it all worthwhile but defies the laws of probability. Call it whatever you like—random accident, multiple coincidence, star-and-planet convergence, fate, blind luck, divine intervention. It happens. It happened to Jake Runyon and me that stormy March night.

An ex-con named Kyle Franklin, not long out of San Quentin after serving six years for armed robbery, decides he wants sole custody of his seven-year-old son. He drags his new girlfriend to San Francisco, where his former wife is raising the boy as a single mom, and beats and threatens the ex-wife and kidnaps the child. Rather than leave the city quick, he decides he needs some sustenance for the long drive to Lila's sister's place in L.A. and stops at the first diner he sees, less than a quarter mile from the ex-wife's apartment building—a diner where two case-hardened private detectives happen to be staked out.

We overhear part of his conversation with Lila and it sounds wrong to us. We notice the blood on his coat sleeve, the scraped knuckles, his prison pallor, the Odin's Cross—a prison tattoo and racist symbol—on his hand, and the fact that he's carrying a concealed weapon. So we follow him outside and brace him, he pulls the gun, and while we're struggling our deadbeat dad chooses that moment to show up. The smart thing for Maxwell to have done was to drive off, avoid trouble; instead he lets his curiosity and arrogance get the best of him, and comes over to watch, and then picks up Franklin's gun and hands it to me nice as you please. And so we foil a kidnapping and collar not one but two violent, abusive fathers in the space of about three minutes.

What are the odds? Astronomical. You could live three or four lifetimes and nothing like it would ever happen again.

It's a little like hitting the megabucks state lottery. That night, Runyon and I were the ones holding the winning ticket.

REVENANT

1

The weirdest damn case I've ever been involved in began, innocuously enough, with a phone call.

I was alone in the agency office when it came in late that May morning, the day being one of the two per week I spend at my desk now that I'm semiretired. Tamara had gone down to the South Park Cafe to get us some take-out lunch, and Jake Runyon and Alex Chavez were both out on field assignments. So the decision to follow up or not follow up was mine to make, and the subsequent investigation mine if and when it came to that.

The caller gave his name as Peter Erskine, his profession as stockbroker and financial advisor, and said that he was calling from his home in Atherton. The location got my attention right away; Atherton is an uber-affluent community on the Peninsula some thirty miles south of San Francisco. His problem, he said, was personal and "very strange and disturbing." When you've been a detective as long as I have, you get so you can read voice nuances over a phone wire. He didn't sound particularly upset, but there was a detectable undercurrent of tension in his businesslike approach—the way a man speaks when he's keeping himself under tight control.

"How do you mean strange, Mr. Erskine?"

"It's . . . complicated, and it takes considerable explaining better done in person. Could you possibly come to my home this afternoon?"

I said, "Our policy with prospective new clients is an initial consultation here in our offices, to determine if our services meet your needs. You understand, I'm sure."

"Yes, of course, but this matter also concerns my wife. She'll want to meet and speak with you as well, but her health is poor and she doesn't travel well. If you could see your way clear to driving down, I'll pay you two hundred and fifty dollars for your time, plus travel expenses, whether you agree to help us or not. In cash if you'd like."

Well, we'd been offered more than that up front, but not very often and not in recent memory. Besides which, the "very strange and disturbing" appellation to his problem was tantalizing, I was not particularly busy, just working a routine employee background check for a large industrial company, and the weather was too unseasonably nice for this time of year to be cooped up inside if you could justify a field trip. Two hundred and fifty bucks plus expenses was plenty enough justification.

I said, "What time would be convenient for you?"

"As soon as you can make it."

"Two o'clock?" I was thinking about my lunch. No breakfast to speak of this morning, and my stomach was grumbling.

"Two o'clock, yes, that's fine. Thank you."

"Address? Phone number in case I should need it?"

He provided them, along with general directions that

weren't necessary. The GPS Kerry had talked me into install-
ing in my car—rightly so, I had to admit, despite my general
dislike of electronic gadgets—would take me to his home by
the shortest possible route.

Tamara came back and into my office as I was ending the
conversation with Peter Erskine. Tamara Corbin, my partner
and just about young enough to be my granddaughter. Whip-
smart and as organized and creative as they come—literally
the guiding hand and beating heart of the agency. When I'd
first hired her for her computer expertise several years back,
I'd been running a modest one-man operation; once she
learned the ropes and took on more and more responsibility,
she'd worked tirelessly to expand the business to the point
where now we employed two full-time field operatives and another on a part-time basis and were dragging down five times
the annual profits I'd made on my own. One of these days,
long after I was gone, she'd undoubtedly head up the largest
investigative agency in the city.

She set one of two Styrofoam sandwich containers on my
desk. Its contents had the warm, spicy aroma of hot pastrami.
"New client?" she asked, nodding at the phone.

"Prospective. Peter Erskine, stockbroker and financial advisor, Atherton."

One of her eyebrows went up at that, climbed another fraction
when I told her about Erskine's cash offer. "Man's serious,
whatever his problem. Could be interesting."

"Could be," I agreed.

Interesting? What a hell of an understatement that turned
out to be.

2

Atherton is one of those expensive, wooded, hillside communities that prides itself on its scenic attractions and considerable amount of open space. The homes in the upper sections below Highway 280 are mostly situated on large parcels shaded by heritage trees and surrounded by lawns and carefully tended gardens. There are quite a few that qualify as estates, tucked away on acres of real estate behind stone walls, ornate fences, high hedges. You could buy yourself one of those for ten million on up to thirty million or more if you were one of the upwardly mobile, mega-rich folk who'd made their pile down in Silicon Valley. Even the less opulent properties would cost you seven figures on the open market.

The property that evidently belonged to Peter Erskine and his wife was modest in comparison to some of its neighbors, probably worth a paltry three or four mil. It had a whitish stone fence and a gated entrance drive, the gates mounted on ornate pillars and open now. I drove on through.

Half an acre of barbered lawn and flowering shrubs separated the house from the road. Two stories of angular modern architecture, faced in the same kind of whitish stone as the fence and decorated at the corners with red fire brick, the house wasn't half as large as most in the vicinity—no more than a dozen rooms, not counting baths. Over on its right side I had a glimpse of a redbrick terrace and, at a distance at the edge of a copse of evergreens, a large hexagonal outbuilding that I would call a gazebo and the Erskines probably labeled a summer-house. There'd be a swimming pool, too, somewhere around back.

The driveway ended in a white-pebbled parking area that would accommodate half a dozen cars. Mine was probably the oldest and cheapest passenger vehicle that had ever been left there. I made my way to the porch and rang the bell. Rolling melody of chimes, footsteps, a pause while I was scrutinized through a peephole magnifier, then a male voice saying my name interrogatively even though it was five minutes of two and I was expected. Erskine being careful nonetheless, for reasons I was about to learn, before he admitted a stranger.

When I confirmed my identity, a chain rattled and he opened up. He was not quite what I expected, but then that's often the case when you form a mental image of someone you've only spoken to on the telephone. I'd figured him for fifty-plus; he was not much older than thirty-five. Casually dressed in a long-sleeved, light blue shirt and fawn-colored slacks. Well set up, fair-haired, strong jawed—not quite pretty-boy handsome but on the cusp. His unsmiling mien, the tight little muscle bulges along his jawline, confirmed the impression I'd had from his phone voice: man under some pressure and determined not to show how much he was affected by it.

If I was not what he'd expected, either—a conservatively dressed man in his mid-sixties instead of your typical young, mod Hollywood version of a private investigator—he gave no indication of it. He thanked me for being prompt, shook my hand, ushered me in and down a long hallway into a large, bright room with two walls of floor-to-ceiling French-style doors and windows that overlooked the terrace and the gazebo/summerhouse in the distance. The terrace wrapped around to the rear, where I could see a lot of white wrought-iron lawn furniture and the glint of sunlight on water. Swimming pool. Right.

On Erskine's invitation I parked myself on one of several red-and-green-patterned chairs. The room, warm from the sun's slanting rays, was decorated strictly according to a woman's taste—the remaining two walls painted a pale yellow, half a dozen whimsical watercolor paintings of elves, gnomes, and leprechauns, lamps with frilly shades, a glass-front display cabinet filled with expensive-looking porcelain and pewter knickknacks. Bright, cheerful elegance, but the kind of room that would make me uncomfortable if I had to spend much time in it.

He didn't immediately sit himself; he went first to the side windows, stood there as if composing himself, then turned abruptly and went to perch stiff backed on a chair facing me.

"This thing that's going on is unnerving enough to me," he said without preamble, "but it's having an even greater effect on Marian, my wife. Her health is fragile as it is. She's resting in the summerhouse now; she likes to spend her afternoons there when the weather's good. We thought it would be best if I spoke to you alone first."

I said, "What is it that's going on, Mr. Erskine?"

"I think my life may be in danger. We both do."

"You think so? You're not sure?"

"Not completely, but there's every indication of it."

"Someone has cause to harm you, is that it?"

"Not as far as I'm concerned. The idea is fantastic."

"A person you know well?"

"A man I never knew at all. What brought us together, if you can call it that, was an accident. And it was *his* fault, not mine."

"What kind of accident?"

"On the freeway, just over a year ago."

"A year is a long time to hold a grudge," I said.

He made a chuckling sound, dry and humorless. "You don't know the half of it yet."

"Did this man threaten you afterward?"

"Yes. Vowed he'd have his revenge."

"In front of witnesses?"

"Yes."

"Make any threats since? Any attempt to carry out his vow?"

Erskine shook his head. Then, "I thought it was all past history until last Friday night."

"What makes you think differently now?"

"There's no other explanation for why I'm suddenly being stalked."

"Stalked? Are you sure?"

"God, yes, I'm sure."

"Have you been to the police?"

"No. There wouldn't be any point in it."

"Why wouldn't there?"

Another headshake.

"Look, Mr. Erskine," I said, "what is it you expect from me? I have to tell you that my agency doesn't do bodyguard work, but I can recommend one that does—"

"No, no, I don't want a bodyguard. There are weapons in

the house, licensed handguns, and I know how to use them. I can take care of myself. I want you to find him, the one who's doing this to me."

"Why a private investigator? Why not the police?"

"Because they wouldn't believe what's been happening, what's behind it, even if I showed them the black host. They'd think Marian and I were imagining things, hallucinating."

"Black host?"

He didn't seem to hear the question. "You may think the same thing—I won't be surprised if you do. But I swear to you, we're not. I've seen him three times now, Marian twice."

"Seen who?"

The humorless synthetic chuckle again; the muscles along Erskine's jawline rippled faintly. "Vok. Antanas Vok."

"And who is he?"

"Not is, *was*. Antanas Vok is dead. He died in a San Jose hospital a year ago last Friday."

3

Several seconds went by while I stared at him. Outside, some kind of bird cut loose with a series of melodious trilling sounds, bright and clear to match the afternoon. Sunlight made golden oblongs of the near side French windows; the places where its rays touched the yellow walls glowed warmly. And here was Peter Erskine, dragging dark shadows into all that cheerful radiance.

I broke the silence finally. "Are you trying to tell me you're being stalked by a dead man?"

"That's how it seems. Marian . . . well, she can't get over the notion that such a thing is possible."

"But you don't believe it?"

"No." But then he pulled back a little by saying, "I sure as hell don't want to believe it."

"Look, Mr. Erskine—"

He asked abruptly, "Do you know what a revenant is?"

"Revenant? No."

"Supposedly it's a spirit come back from the dead in human form."

". . . What, like a zombie?"

"No. A zombie is a mindless corpse risen from the grave. A revenant . . ." He nibbled briefly at his lower lip, then expelled a sighing breath. "A revenant, according to folklore, is the spirit of an evil person with a malevolent purpose—to terrorize and destroy the living."

I said slowly, "That's a pretty incredible notion."

"I know it. It's Marian's, not mine. She has always had a fascination with the occult. When she was a girl she thought she might have psychic powers. She studied parapsychology, joined one of those psychic research outfits—still contributes money to it. Later on she developed an interest in witchcraft and black magic. Not that she actually believes in such things as revenants, let's just say she's susceptible to supernatural possibilities. Obviously I'm not. Whoever is stalking me is a living person, somebody in whatever nut group Vok belonged to. That's why I asked you here, why I want to hire you. To find out who and why at this late date."

I'd been on the verge of getting up and getting out of there. Over the years I've dealt with more than my share of eccentrics, weirdos, smart-ass cuties, and plain crazies, but Erskine did not appear to fit into any of those categories; he seemed straightforward, worried, concerned for his wife if not himself. As long as he didn't expect me to go chasing after phantoms, I was willing to listen to the rest of his story.

I said, "Let me get all of this straight. You had no connection with this Antanas Vok until the freeway accident?"

"I never knew he existed until that day."

"Who was he?"

Erskine's mouth bent into a grimace. "A butcher. In more ways than one, probably."

"What does that mean?"

Headshake.

"All right," I said. "You've seen somebody three times now who resembles Vok?"

"Enough to be recognizable even at night. Size, height, Vandyke beard, burning stare, clothing . . . all the same."

"These sightings took place where?"

"Here, two times when Marian and I were together. The first on the side terrace just outside those windows there, around ten Friday evening. The other time we were having coffee by the pool when he appeared."

"Was anyone else present either time?"

"No. Just the two of us."

"You don't have live-in help?"

"No. A gardener, a part-time cleaning woman, and a full-time cook, but none of them is here in the evenings."

"You say this intruder appeared. How do you mean?"

"As if he'd materialized out of thin air," Erskine said. "I'm not kidding. One second he was there, the next . . . gone. Vanished."

"What exactly did he do each time?"

"Pointed and stared hate at me."

"That's all? No threatening moves?"

"No, but the implied threat was plain enough. I don't frighten easily, neither does Marian, but the way he looked, his face and hands . . . Frankly, it made my blood run cold."

"What about his face and hands?"

The muscles along Erskine's jawline rippled again. "They were more bone than flesh. Like a skeleton's. And there was a kind of eerie glow about him. Ectoplasmic, Marian called it."

"Did he speak at all?"

"No."

"How was he dressed?"

"The same as the day of the accident. Shabby black suit and black hat. But the clothing was all torn up, filthy with what seemed to be dirt."

"Each time you saw him?"

"Yes."

"Did he leave any traces behind? Footprints or the like?"

"No. I looked everywhere on the property, but there was nothing to find. Except . . ."

"Except?"

"A lingering smell. Faint the first time, but last night it was stronger."

"What sort of smell?"

"Nauseating. Like something dead and decayed."

Well, hell. "That kind of stench can be faked," I said. "So can the skeletal resemblance to Vok and the unearthly glow and the rest of it. Stage effects."

"I know. But it was damned realistic nonetheless."

There was nothing supernatural about the vanishing act, either, I thought. With climbable fencing and all the shrubbery and trees on the property, it wouldn't have been too difficult for a man, the living, breathing variety, to trespass more or less unnoticed. Still, there should have been some signs of his presence. Erskine must have missed seeing them in the darkness.

"Where was the third sighting?" I asked.

"Out on the road near the front gate, two nights ago, as I was leaving for a meeting in Palo Alto. He was just standing there, pointing and hating the way he did in the hospital. By the time I stopped the car and got out, he was gone. Vanished, like before."

"The hospital, you said. Was that where Vok made his threat against your life?"

"Yes. The day after the accident, just before he died."

"You went to see him there? Why?"

"One of the doctors called and said he was asking for me. I didn't want to go, but Marian talked me into it. Act of compassion. Honoring a dying man's last request." Erskine's mouth quirked. "Softhearted, that's my Marian. A trait I'd always admired in her before."

"Did she go with you?"

"Yes. She saw Vok grab my hand and put that thing into it—"

"Thing?"

"—and heard him swear his sick vengeance. So did a nurse and another man who was in the room."

"A member of Vok's family?"

"I don't know who he was. Possibly somebody from the coven or whatever it was they were involved with."

"Coven?"

"You know, witchcraft."

"Now what are you telling me? That Vok was some kind of devil worshipper?"

"That's exactly what he was. He as much as said so, a lot of crap about Satan being his lord and master. That's why Marian believes the revenant thing is conceivable."

I had another urge to haul my carcass out of there. But it passed and I stayed put. There's a kind of perverse fascination in stories like the one Erskine was spinning for me; the more fantastic they are, the greater the lure to hear them all the way through. I'm too practical minded to give credence to evil spirits wreaking vengeance from beyond the grave, but there's no denying the existence of devil worship. Or that there are credulous people who buy into the whole occult shtick. Marian Erskine seemed to be one of those, even if her husband shared my skepticism.

"Look," he said, "I know how crazy all of this sounds, but it's true, everything I've told you. A newspaper reporter found out about the threat and claimed to have dug up information proving that both Vok and his wife belonged to a devil cult. He tried to interview Marian and me. I wouldn't let him in the house."

"Did he publish a story anyway?"

"Not that I know of. If I'd seen one, you can bet I'd have gone straight to our lawyers."

"Remember his name? Or what paper he was with?"

"Not his name. The San Jose paper, I think it was."

I said, "Tell me about the traffic accident. How did it happen?"

"Vok's reckless driving. On the freeway near downtown San Jose. I was down there on a business matter, about to exit, when he veered over in front of me so suddenly he clipped my front fender. The impact spun us both around. I was lucky, my 'Vette stayed upright and all I got were some bruises and a cracked wristbone, but Vok's van flipped and rolled and slammed into the overpass abutment. His wife was killed instantly. They got him out alive but in critical condition. He was barely hanging on when Marian and I saw him in the hospital the next day. Lived just long enough to swear his revenge."

"What was your reaction to that?"

"It didn't bother me very much—just a dying lunatic's delusion. Marian was shocked and scared at the time, and even more upset and afraid for me when the reporter confirmed what Vok was into. But over time, when nothing happened, she got over it. Until last Friday."

"One year from the date of the accident."

"From the date of Vok's death, actually."

"How do you account for the passage of so much time before these recent sightings?"

"I can't account for it," Erskine said. "Marian says the revenant might have had difficulty crossing back from the Other Side, but that's bunk. The only rational explanation I can think of is that there's some kind of anniversary connection."

"Somebody involved with this devil cult carrying out Vok's threat."

"Yes. The man in the hospital room must have told them about it."

"Could he be the one impersonating Vok?"

"No. Vok was short, slight, in his fifties. The other man was tall, heavyset, years younger."

"Did he give his name?"

"He never said a word."

"Would you know if he's the one who claimed Vok's body? And the wife's?"

"No idea."

"You said something earlier about a 'thing' Vok thrust into your hand. What did you mean?"

The question produced another grimace. "A damned black host."

"That's the second time you've used that term. Explain it."

"Better if I let it explain itself." Erskine slid a hand inside his jacket, brought out a plain white business envelope, then stood to pass it to me. "Careful when you touch the thing. It leaves a residue on your fingers."

The envelope was unsealed and nearly weightless. Inside was a solid black disc about the size of a poker chip. I upended it into my palm. It appeared to be made of some brittle, grainy substance, and there were three tiny triangular horns that gave it the look of a gear with most of its teeth missing. There were also shallow indentations and a shallow piece missing along the opposite edge. Bite marks.

Erskine said, "I assume from your name that you're Catholic, so I guess you know what it is."

Yeah, I knew. It was a perversion of the host, the body of Christ, used in Catholic communion—a black host for a black mass. Even though I no longer embraced the faith, this thing had an unclean feel on my skin. I dumped it back into the envelope, tossed the envelope on the floor. A few tiny grains of black stained my palm; I scrubbed it off on the knee of my pants, kept scrubbing even after the residue no longer adhered to the skin.

"Where did you get it?"

"It was on the floor in the hall Friday night," Erskine said. "Must've been slipped under the door."

"Before or after the Vok figure appeared?"

"Probably before. Marian found it the next morning."

"It couldn't be the same host Vok shoved into your hand in the hospital?"

"Hardly. I threw that one in the garbage as soon as we left the room, for Marian's sake as much as for mine. It . . . well, you can imagine how frightened she was. To her it meant Vok really was in league with the devil, that he was capable of using the powers of darkness to destroy me, perhaps even to . . ." He let the rest of the sentence hang.

"To what?"

"Steal my soul."

More supernatural nonsense. "Come on now, Mr. Erskine."

"That's Marian's perception, not mine."

"How does she imagine something like that could happen?"

"I think you'd better ask her."

4

We went out through the side French doors onto the terrace, angled across it and along a wide brick path to the summerhouse. It was as large as a bandstand, surmounted by a dome with little windows in it and partially shaded by a half circle of evergreens; four of its hexagonal openings were covered now by rattan shades. Purple and white flowering shrubs flanked the entrance to a waist-high level; their mingled scents were sweet on the balmy spring air. The structure's position was such that the woman sitting inside wasn't visible until Erskine and I had gone two-thirds of the way across the lawn, and it was only when we stepped up inside that I had a clear look at her.

She was not what I'd expected, either. Something of a surprise, in fact. At least a dozen years older than her husband, maybe more; it was difficult to tell because the dusky light in there veiled her face and upper body. Even so, it was obvious that she was in poor health. Small, frail—she could not have weighed more than a hundred pounds. Pale, blotchy skin. Too-red lipstick that gave her mouth the look of a bloody slash. Hair a dark auburn, expertly dyed and cut. Earlobes

185

heavy with diamond earrings. The smoothness of her cheeks and forehead indicated a facelift or two, but when she leaned forward into a shaft of sunlight I saw dark smudges under her eyes and lines like tiny fissures radiating out from around her mouth.

A thick-cushioned chaise lounge, one of several pieces of wrought-iron furniture that matched the ones on the terrace, was what she was reclining on. On a low table at her side were a cut-glass crystal decanter and tumbler, both half-full of what might have been brandy. Even though no breeze stirred the warm air in there, her torso was wrapped in a heavy knit sweater and a patterned afghan covered her from the waist down.

Erskine went to her, laid a solicitous hand on her shoulder; she reached up to cover it with one of her own as he introduced us. The look of him standing there put the words *trophy husband* into my head. Well, why not? That kind of marriage happens often enough among the rich, trophy husbands as well as trophy wives.

Marian Erskine let me have her other hand; it felt thin and dry in mine, like old seamed leather. But when she said, "Thank you for coming," her voice was a strong contralto that belied her fragile appearance. However much of the liquor she'd had, it hadn't affected her speech or dulled her large, dark eyes. Her gaze was steady, direct, without any discernible sign of pain or distress.

"Peter explained everything to you? In detail?"

Erskine said, "Just as we discussed, Marian," and I said, "Yes."

"And you're still here." She made a sound that might have

been intended as a laugh but came out as a dry cough. "I was afraid it would all sound so bizarre to a man in your profession that you wouldn't want anything to do with us."

"I deal in facts, Mrs. Erskine. But I try to keep an open mind."

"That's all we ask. You will help us, then?"

"I have some more questions before I make a commitment."

"Of course you do. About my concerns that there may be a supernatural explanation for what has been happening—that Antanas Vok's revenant has returned to carry out his vengeance against my husband."

"Yes."

"Peter dismisses it as utter nonsense."

"That's not quite true," Erskine said. He seemed less in command in her presence, almost defensive. "I have an open mind, too; you know that, Marian. It's just that—"

"Just that you don't share my regard for the paranormal. Well, you're no different from most people." She looked at me again. "I'm not what you'd call a true believer, either, you know—that is, one who embraces all aspects of the paranormal and supernatural without question. I have many questions, many doubts. My interest in the occult is more academic than anything else, though I suppose Peter told you that when I was younger I believed for a time that I had a psychic gift."

I nodded, and she went on, "There are enough documented cases of preternatural phenomena throughout history to have blunted if not completely destroyed my skepticism. I very much want Peter to be right that what we've seen is a living person guised as Antanas Vok, not his evil spirit returned from the Other Side. But until that is proven to my satisfaction, I can't and won't discount the revenant possibility."

I said I understood. "About Vok. You had no idea of his beliefs until the incident in the hospital?"

"None whatsoever. That he was a practicing Satanist and I have some knowledge of the black arts is a macabre coincidence."

"About this revenant concept. Is such a spirit supposed to have physical powers? Could one, for instance, carry around an object such as the black host you found?"

"I can't answer that with any certainty, of course," she said, "but I would think that it is possible. The powers of darkness are considerable, much stronger than we can possibly imagine. Physical objects surely can be made to materialize if not actually carried."

"How would a revenant go about harming a living person?"

"There are a number of ways. One would be to haunt his victim openly, terrorize him until he sickens and dies."

"Like a voodoo curse is supposed to work?"

"Yes, though without such trappings as pins and dolls."

Erskine said, "That wouldn't have any effect on me. You have to believe in that kind of thing before it can harm you."

"Don't be too sure, Peter."

"What are the other ways?" I asked.

Marian Erskine gave another dry cough, reached over to pick up her glass and sip from it. "Cognac," she said when she put it down. "I shouldn't, but it steadies my nerves."

"Not too much," he warned her. "You know what the doctor said—"

"Damn the doctor!" she said with such sudden vehemence that it started her coughing again. "And don't treat me like an invalid child; you know how I detest that." She pushed his hand off her shoulder, helped herself to another sip of cognac. He backed off a step, looking hurt.

I said to prompt her, "Other ways, Mrs. Erskine?"

"Possession," she said.

"Possession. You mean the spirit enters the body of the victim, takes control of it?"

"The victim, or someone else weak willed enough to do the spirit's bidding. A temporary host, you see? Signified, perhaps, by the appearance of the devil's symbol, a black host."

"If it's the victim who's possessed, then what? How would the spirit destroy him?"

"Theft of the soul is the most diabolical method."

". . . I don't understand that."

"A basic tenet of black magic is the belief that the soul is not just the essence of life, but a literal indwelling object—a kind of homunculus that can be seized from within and then taken away. Once this happens, the mortal body collapses and soon withers and dies."

"Is there another method?"

"A more immediate one, yes. By seizing control of the victim's will, forcing him to destroy himself by his own hand."

Gruesome stuff, a mixture of primitive fear, skewed logic, and perverted religious doctrine. You couldn't have paid me enough to buy into it for five seconds. Erskine, either, if he were pressed, judging from the dispassionate look he directed my way from his stance behind her chaise lounge. His wife claimed only academic interest in the black arts, and yet she seemed even paler now and her hand was unsteady as she lifted the decanter and splashed more cognac into her glass. If not a true believer, then close to it—and considerably disturbed by the events of the past few days.

Erskine put a hand on her shoulder again. "Please, Marian, no more alcohol. It's not good for your heart."

She ignored him. Down the new pour went, in two convulsive gulps. The cognac made her cough again, seemed to shorten her breath a little, but did nothing to improve her color.

"Is there anything more you'd like to know?" she asked me. Irritation toward me in her voice now. "About evil spirits, black mass rituals, the Witches' Sabbath, the signing of convenants with the devil—"

"No. That's not necessary. I've heard enough."

She seemed to realize she might have spoken too harshly; she pasted on a smile and said in a more even tone, "What I've told you hasn't changed your mind, has it? About helping us?"

In spite of my skepticism, the conversation had made me feel just a little uncomfortable. Out of my element in a case like this. Once again I had an impulse to back off and back out, but the pleading in Mrs. Erskine's voice, the nervous tension in her body and veiled fear in her eyes, overrode my better judgment. The thing was, I felt sorry for her. And whatever was going on here had a rational, not a supernatural, explanation, and that I could deal with. Up to a point, anyway.

"No," I said, "I haven't changed my mind. But I can't promise you results, Mrs. Erskine. It's been a year since the accident and the Voks' death and there's not much to go on. All I can guarantee you is that I'll do my best on your behalf."

"That is all we expect."

Erskine asked her if she wanted to go back to the house; she said no, she'd stay there a while longer. "Not with the cognac," he said, and plucked the decanter off the table. She gave him a dark look but not an argument, and dismissed him, and me, by closing her eyes.

He and I returned to the sunroom, where he wrote me a hefty retainer check that included, at his insistence, the $250 he'd promised me for the drive down and consultation. I asked him a few more questions while he was doing that, but the answers weren't useful. He didn't know where the Voks had lived. Or the name of the doctor who'd called with the dying man's request. Or the name of the nurse who'd been in the room when the black host was passed and the vow made. And he couldn't remember anything more about the friend or relative of the Voks who'd been there.

On my way back to the city I mentally replayed the interviews with Erskine and his wife. The more I went over them, the more surreal they seemed. Devil cults. Black hosts. Soul-stealing evil spirits from beyond the grave. This was the twenty-first century, for God's sake. Such things couldn't possibly exist in the modern world.

No, but evil sure as hell did. You had only to look at the media any day, every day, for proof of that. All kinds of evil, all kinds of noxious acts. Some of it had touched me before, in various ways. Hurt people I liked and respected, hurt me and those I loved.

One other thing for certain: whatever I did for the Erskines, however far I went with an investigation, I would not let that happen again.

5

It was a little past five when the heavy freeway and city traffic finally allowed me to return to South Park and the agency offices. As per usual, Tamara was still at her desk; close of business to her, most days, was six at the earliest and sometimes seven or eight if she had enough work to keep her that long. Saturdays included, now that she was between male companions. As young as she was, fifty-to-sixty-hour weeks was a punishing schedule and potentially damaging to her health as well as her social life. I'd tried to convince her to ease off a little, to no avail. She was stubborn and ambitious and genuinely passionate about her job. Hell, I knew all about that kind of attitude. I'd been a workaholic myself back in the day.

"How'd it go down in rich folks' country?" she asked when I walked into her office. "Peter Erskine's problem something for us?"

"Not really, but I'm going to look into it anyway. Against my better judgment."

"Yeah? How come?"

"The problem, Erskine's and his wife's, is more than just strange. It's plain crazy weird."

"Crazy weird how?"

"You're going to have as much trouble believing this as I did," I said, and went on to give her a capsule rundown of the two interviews. Right: she had trouble believing it.

"Oh, man! Devil worship? Some freakin' zombie looking to steal somebody's soul?"

"Not a zombie, a so-called revenant. Evil spirit in human form."

"Whatever. Can't tell me you bought any of that supernatural stuff."

"No, but whatever's going on has got both of them spooked—no pun intended. Erskine's the one being stalked, but she's taking it the hardest."

"You think whoever's pretending to be this Vok character is connected to the devil cult?"

"That would seem to be the most logical explanation. If there is a devil cult."

"So why wait a year to carry out the deathbed vow? And why not just off him and get it over with, instead of skulking around at night pointing fingers and smelling like he just crawled out of a cemetery?"

"Good questions. Mrs. Erskine thinks the delay has something to do with the anniversary of Vok's death. Maybe. The skulking and the holding off . . . scare tactics, to let Erskine know he's a marked man. Again, maybe."

"You really want to go ahead with an investigation, huh?"

I laid Erskine's retainer check on her desk. "Here's one reason."

"But not the only one. You taught me never take on a case just for money unless there's a financial need, and we're so far in the black right now we're heading into another tax bracket."

"Chalk it up to curiosity."

"Yeah, the morbid kind."

"And to the reason why we're in business—helping people in trouble."

"Uh-huh."

There was a fourth reason that I'd admitted to myself on the drive back to the city, but that I would not tell Tamara, or Kerry when I got home, or anybody else. Boredom, plain and simple. Nearly all of my investigative work these days was done on the phone—insurance fraud claims, skip-traces, deadbeat dad jobs, employee background checks, arrangements for process serving. Routine, for the most part. And on the four or five days a week when I wasn't in the office, I spent more time rattling around looking for things to occupy my time than I did enjoying myself; you can only do so much reading, and my collection of pulp magazines was about as complete as it was likely to get given what 1920s and 1930s issues of *Black Mask* and other rare titles were going for these days. Mostly I was okay with the semiretired lifestyle, but now and then it grew a little stale, made me feel out of touch and unneeded. This was one of those times.

"So okay," Tamara said. "You want me to run a back-grounder on this Vok character, right?"

"Right. Him and his wife both. On the Erskines, too—anything that might have a bearing on this revenge thing." We didn't usually conduct background checks on clients without a compelling reason, but this was anything but an ordinary case. The more information I had, the better idea I would have of how to proceed.

"What else?"

I consulted my notes. Jake Runyon, Alex Chavez, and most

other private operatives these days carry voice-activated devices to record client interviews, but I still use the old-fashioned method of writing down information in a private brand of shorthand. Truth is, I have an uneasy, need-hate relationship with modern technology. There's no question that computers, Internet search engines, iPhones and iPads, and GPS systems are useful tools that make detective work and some aspects of life easier; but they're also responsible for a considerable amount of negative change, chiefly the obliteration of personal privacy. The gadgets cluttering up my life are necessary sometimes, but I use them as sparingly as possible. Old habits are hard to break when a dinosaur like me gets into his so-called "golden years."

"Whatever you can pull up on the freeway accident that started all this," I said in answer to Tamara's question. "Also the name of the San Jose reporter who found out about the alleged devil worship connection and tried to interview the Erskines."

"That should be easy enough, if he worked for the *Mercury News*."

"Other IDs, too, if possible: the doctor who attended Vok, the nurse and the other man who were in the hospital room, and the person or persons who claimed the bodies of Vok and his wife."

"Not so easy. Hospital records are pretty hard to access without covert hacking."

"Do what you have to, within reason," I said. "But I don't want to know the specifics."

Tamara flashed me one of her sly grins. "Want me to get on this right away?"

"Tomorrow morning's soon enough. It's five-thirty. Why don't you knock off early for a change?"

"No reason to. All that's waiting for me in my flat is some leftover Chinese takeout and a bathroom that needs cleaning. Besides, I've got plenty of other work to do."

"Not overloading you, am I?"

"Hah. Couldn't if you tried. Only thing I'd rather do is screw, and I can't even do that now that that asshole Horace and me busted up again. Or get next to Mr. V anymore. He went and died on me and I haven't had a chance to replace him."

I sighed and beat a hasty retreat into my own office. I did not want to hear any more about Mr. V for vibrator, dead or alive. Tamara's insistence on sharing intimate details about her sex life, or lack thereof, was one of her less than endearing traits.

I did not tell Kerry about my interviews with Peter and Marian Erskine. Most of the time I confided in her whenever a provocative new case had my attention, just as she confided in me when there were interesting developments at Bates and Carpenter, the ad agency where she was now a vice president in charge of several accounts. But not this case.

It wasn't that she would have openly disapproved of my decision to take it on, though she might have questioned the wisdom of it. It would have been an act of cruelty to bring disturbing topics like devil cults and black hosts and vengeful spirits into my home. It was one thing to deal with such matters professionally, where you could employ a certain amount of detachment, another to subject Kerry—and possibly my inquisitive fourteen-year-old adopted daughter, Emily—to any of the nasty details.

What I did do, after dinner, was boot up my laptop and conduct a little private Internet research into the history of Satanic worship—as much of it as I could stand to read. The practice had started among primitive peoples in all corners of the earth, I learned, a reverse worship engaged in when fertility rites failed and prayers to benign gods went unanswered. When that happened, some of those primitive races—ancient Babylonians and Druids, among others—appealed instead to the dark gods through virgin sacrifices and other blasphemies.

From the Dark Ages onward, all sorts of sorcerers and sorceresses joined in the Sabbat, or Witches' Sabbath, to perform black masses and attempt to summon demons and make covenants with Satan. Human life was cheap in those days, and in the centuries that followed; people vanished without much effort to find out what had happened to them, especially when members of the nobility indulged in the black arts—human monsters like the Marquis de Sade, Gilles de Rais, Madame de Montespan.

There didn't seem to be much doubt that devil worship continues to exist in these so-called enlightened times. Communicants, as they were called, were still being drawn into witch cults by the freedom to indulge in forbidden practices under the guise of ritual: sexual orgies, blood sacrifices, the black mass communion of drinking of real blood instead of consecrated wine, reading scripture backward, hanging crucifixes upside down. Crazy shit, as Tamara would have termed it. The communicants were of three general types: those who weren't smart enough to know better, those who got a sick thrill out of sacrilegious ceremony, and those who were addicted to orgies and/or ritual killing. Which had Antanas Vok and his wife been? I wondered.

By the time I quit reading, I was having some second thoughts about cashing Peter Erskine's retainer check and going ahead with the investigation. This case was like nothing in my experience. Grotesque, disturbing. I could still see that damned black host, still feel it unclean in the palm of my hand—a genuine symbol of evil. It was as if it had left a permanent invisible stain. Ridiculous thought, brought on by too much imagination and heightened by my Catholic upbringing, but it lingered nonetheless.

I wrestled with my feelings, and professionalism won. When I make a commitment, I honor it. I kept remembering the palpable tension and fear in Marian Erskine, too—fear for her husband's life, fear of being at the mercy of unknown forces. The one sure way to dispel her superstitious concerns about revenants and the powers of darkness was to prove the threat human by exposing the person or persons behind it.

Still, I had the nagging thought that I'd gotten myself into something I didn't completely understand and that one day, no matter what the outcome, I would come to regret it.

6

Tamara had already pulled up some of the information I'd requested when I arrived at the agency the next morning. It was only nine o'clock, so she must have come in early. She looked tired, her dark brown face drawn and the whites of her eyes streaked with faint red lines. Not getting enough sleep. And not eating much or well; she'd lost more weight recently than was good for a young woman with her large-boned body. Overwork, and the second difficult breakup with her cello-playing boyfriend, Horace Fields. But there was nothing I could say or do about it. She was as independent as they come. The only advice from me she'd take to heart was the professional kind, and sometimes only after an argument.

"Not too much on the Voks—wife's name Elza—or the accident that you don't already know," she told me. "The reporter is a dude named Lenihan, first name Joseph. Only he doesn't and never did work for the *Mercury News*. Freelancer for any newspaper or other publication that'll run one of his creature features."

"His what?"

"Far-out stuff. You know, weird happenings, unexplained phenomena, that kind of thing."

"Sort of like Charles Fort."

"Who?"

Young people today: no sense of history. "Never mind."

"Well, anyway," Tamara said, "if he wrote up the hospital revenge incident, none of the mainstream print media would touch it. Might've gotten it into some supermarket sheet, but if so I couldn't find a reference through any of the search engines."

"Potential legal problem even if real names weren't used."

"Right. But the good news is that Lenihan also writes a creature-feature blog called 'Oddments' and he posted a long piece there. You can say pretty much anything you want online if you don't cross the libel line. No names in the piece, but there're enough details to ID what he's writing about. You'll see. I printed it out for you."

"Good, thanks. Anything else?"

"A little on the Erskines, yeah," she said. "Still working on the other stuff you asked for. All I've got so far is the name of the hospital—South Bay Memorial."

"What should I know about the Erskines?"

"Not much that I can see. Marian Erskine's estimated worth is around fifteen mil. Inherited money—her father was an electrical engineer, invented some kind of device that he patented and sold to the aerospace industry for megabucks back in the seventies. She's fifty-one, married and divorced twice before she hooked up with Peter Erskine. He's lasted the longest so far—six years. No children. Longtime member of a group called the International Psychical Research Society; makes an annual four-figure donation to it. Used to be proactive in charity work before her heart attack."

"Heart attack? When was that?"

"Three months ago. Bad one—she nearly died."

No wonder she looked as she did, why Erskine was so solicitous and disapproving of her cognac drinking. Alcohol coupled with nervous tension and undue excitement is a potentially lethal combination in a heart patient. But I wondered why neither of them had mentioned the coronary to me. Too painful and too personal a subject, maybe. And irrelevant to the task I was being hired for.

"Peter Erskine," Tamara said. "Age thirty-six. Born and raised in Los Gatos. No prior marriages. Went to work for a brokerage firm in Silicon Valley straight out of high school, worked his way up to a low-level sales position. Met Marian Erskine at a charity tennis tournament at one of the country clubs down there—he plays and so did she before the heart thing. Not long after they were married, he opened his own business—stockbroker and financial advisor—with her backing. Doesn't seem to've made much of a success at it. Has an office with one employee in Menlo Park."

"He's a good-looking guy. And she's considerably older and in poor health. How good is the marriage?"

"You mean is he the type to put his balls in other courts?" I winced at that, and she grinned. "Well, I don't know, I didn't do any digging along those lines. But if a young guy's not getting much at home, wouldn't be any surprise if he went out prowling now and then. Real careful like, though. Wouldn't want to lose his meal ticket."

"Don't be so cynical."

"Hah," she said.

I took the thin sheaf of printouts she handed me into my office and sat at my desk to go over them. I skimmed through

a couple of brief newspaper accounts of the fatal freeway accident. Erskine's version, that Vok had caused it by inattentive
driving, was corroborated by witnesses. Vok had been taken
to and had died in South Bay Memorial Hospital, the reason
for that destination being twofold: it was relatively close to the
scene of the accident and it had a trauma unit.

The background info on the Voks was scanty, evidently all
that was available; Tamara is nothing if not thorough. He'd
been fifty-two, his wife forty-nine, at the time of their deaths.
Both of Lithuanian descent. Antanas (Lithuanian for *Anthony*)
Vok had been born in the Baltic state and immigrated to
the U.S. with mother and father, now both deceased, at age
twelve, and as an adult had become a naturalized citizen; Elza
Vok had been born in this country. No children. Next of kin
unknown. They'd lived at 1936 Dillard Street #4 in San Jose,
where he'd worked as a butcher for one of the medium-sized
supermarket chains and she as a cleaning woman. Nothing on
their religious beliefs or alleged cult ties, of course. Devotees of
witchcraft and black magic don't advertise the fact.

The printout on our clients contained a few more details,
such as Peter Erskine's office address and the name of his sole
employee, a woman named Melanie Vinson, but none that
held my attention. Joseph Lenihan's blog write-up did.

The header on it was "Dead Men Rise Up Never?" The
tone of the piece was a curious mix of flip-hip—the kind of
wry light touch reporters gave to "silly season" stories back in
the day—and serious occult-themed speculation. Lenihan's
style, I supposed, for all his blog entries. No names were used,
as Tamara had said, just terms such as "accident victim of Eu-
ropean descent" and "prominent Peninsula resident." Antanas
Vok's last words to Peter Erskine were quoted verbatim:

"I will return from the dead and destroy you as you have destroyed me. You will die a death far more terrible than mine. This I vow in the name of Satan, my lord and master, with whom I have made an eternal covenant." The passing of the black host was also mentioned in some detail.

Lenihan went on to say that, according to the unnamed "reliable source" he'd gotten this information from, the recipient and his wife were "consumed with terror and immediately fled the room" and that later they had "refused all requests for an interview about the incident." He then wrote: "Subsequent investigation revealed undeniable evidence that the dead man worshipped the devil and took part in Satanic rituals and blow-your-mind sex orgies." And finished up with: "Is it possible that a dead dude in league with Lucifer can wreak vengeance on the living? Only time will tell."

Assuming the Vok quote was accurate, and it probably was since Lenihan also knew about the black host, the "reliable source" had to be somebody who was in the hospital room at the time. The nurse Erskine had mentioned? Or had Lenihan managed to track down the tall, heavyset, stoic party related to or acquainted with the Voks?

The "undeniable evidence" verifying the devil worship was given as "a bone-freezing collection of grimoires, drawings of pentagrams and other black magic symbols, correspondence describing blood sacrifices, and other weird de Sade type stuff." Some of the titles of the grimoires, or manuals for invoking demons and spirits of the dead, were listed: *Malleus Maleficarum. The Golden Bough. The Book of Eibon. The Grimoire of Pope Honorius.* And two in German, which apparently Vok had been conversant in: *Die Walpurgisnacht im Westphalialeben* and *Den Nederwelt von Renaissanischer Zeit.*

How Lenihan knew all this wasn't stated, though there was a sly inference that he'd managed to gain access to the couple's apartment after Vok's death, just long enough to view its contents and take some notes. Whether he'd also appropriated any of the books or other items was an unanswered question. He did say that all of the evidence "mysteriously disappeared shortly afterward," the inference there being that he'd gone back for a second look and found the apartment cleaned out.

That was all. Anything more I would have to try to pry out of Lenihan himself. If I could get him to talk to me in the first place.

The address Tamara had found for him was in Santa Clara, north of San Jose; she'd also gotten his telephone number. A page of background info told me he was forty years old, unmarried, and—no surprise—a pothead with one arrest for possession, another plus a hand-slap conviction for minor dealing. Writing creature features was apparently an avocation; his main source of income came from repairing computers for college students and others who couldn't afford topline service, work he did from home.

I pulled the desk phone over and tapped out his number. The voice that answered said, "Lenihan's Service, at your service," in a slow and mellow drawl, as if he might already be a little stoned.

I gave him my name, nothing more, and asked if he'd be home for the next couple of hours. He said, "No plans to go anywhere. Computer problem? I specialize in PCs, but I do Macs, too."

"We can discuss the problem when I get there. Hour, hour and fifteen minutes okay?"

"Any time. I'll be here."

7

Santa Clara is another upscale South Bay community, not as affluent as Atherton but still a desirable nesting place for what's left of the upper middle class. It's also the new home of what used to be the San Francisco 49ers. I say used to be because many of the homegrown city dwellers like me who loyally supported the team at Kezar and Candlestick for decades were none too happy with the move forty-three miles south to the glitzy new, superexpensive, poorly situated Levi's Stadium—a stadium that could have and should have been built on available city land next to AT&T Park in downtown S.F.

Sure, winning the bid to host the 2016 Super Bowl was a major coup for the organization and a financial boon for San Francisco despite the South Bay location of the game. But that's not enough to mollify me and many of the other faithful in the city and the North Bay. If anything, it makes the move seem even more of a defection, a fan-base shift that amounts to a collective slap in the face of the old guard. As far as we're concerned, the ownership should be forced to drop *San Francisco* from the team name and replace it with something generic

and more honest—the Golden State 49ers, for instance, following the lead of the pro basketball franchise when the Warriors
quit playing their games in the city back in 1971.

As fashionable as most of Santa Clara is, it has its pockets of
lower-income housing. Joe Lenihan lived in one of these, in a
nondescript apartment house not far off the 101 freeway. His
unit was on the second floor, rear. I rang his bell, identified
myself when his voice came over the intercom, and he said,
"Come on up; door's open," and buzzed me in.

The front section of what was probably his apartment's
living room had been turned into a kind of business anteroom
by the addition of wall-to-wall blue curtains. The space was
crammed with two tables and two chairs facing each other
across the larger table. A couple of desktop PCs and a laptop
wearing name tags sat on the smaller table, evidently repaired
and awaiting customer pickup.

A couple of seconds after I entered, the curtains parted and
I had my first look at Joe Lenihan. He wasn't what I'd expected any more than Peter Erskine had been. The image I'd
had was of a bearded, somewhat scruffy neo-hippie reeking of
pot smoke. He was the antithesis of that: clean-shaven, with
gray-flecked brown hair trimmed short and clear hazel eyes;
dressed in a loose sport shirt and corduroys that were old and
somewhat frayed but clean. And not even a stray whiff of
marijuana came from him or from behind the curtains. You'd
think that at my age and as many years as I've been in business, I would know better than anyone not to fall into the
preconceived-notion trap.

He had a welcoming smile for me, but it dimmed somewhat
when he saw that my hands were empty. "No computer?

I don't sell them, you know, just repair them." I'd been wrong about his voice, too: slow and mellow was apparently his natural way of speaking.

"Computers isn't the reason I'm here, Mr. Lenihan."

"No?" His expression brightened again. "You wouldn't be connected with the media, would you? Come to offer me a writing gig?"

"Sorry, no," I said, and then lied a little. "But I've read your blog."

"Well, one of the chosen few. A pleasure." The smile tilted a little, self-deprecatingly. "Assuming you don't have a complaint about one of my entries, that is."

"No complaints. Just some questions about a particular piece you wrote last year."

"Which one?"

"The one called 'Dead Men Rise Up Never?' About the devil-worshipping accident victim and his deathbed vow."

"Oh, sure. Real weird true story. What about it?"

"I'd like some information on your sources."

Lenihan had beetling brows; one of them arched upward into a boomerang shape over a narrowed eye. The upcurve of his mouth was wary now. "Why? After all this time?"

"Professional reasons." I showed him the photostat of my license.

The other eyebrow humped up to make two boomerangs. The smile stayed, the wariness vanished. "No shit," he said in a pleased sort of way. "How come a private eye's interested in devil worshippers?"

"Not that per se, just Antanas Vok and the cult he belonged to."

"Antanas Vok. So you know his name." Then, eagerly, "Why do you want to know my sources? Who're you working for?"

"That's confidential."

"The guy in Atherton? Did something happen to him?"

"Confidential."

"Yeah, well, so are my sources." Pause. "But maybe we could work something out. What's in it for me if I tell you?"

"Satisfaction in helping solve the problem I'm investigating."

"Hah."

"All right. How about twenty bucks?"

"Well, I can always use extra cash," Lenihan said, "but I can use a good story more. Maybe you don't know it, but I'm kind of a jack-of-all-trades. Freelance journalist as well as blogger and computer repairman."

"Uh-huh. But all I can let you have is the twenty."

"Not even a little something I can build a story on?"

"Not even a hint."

He thought it over, nibbling on a corner of his lower lip. Pretty soon he said, "Well, what the hell. Make it fifty bucks and you've got a deal."

"Fifty's a little steep."

"Not for what I have to tell you."

"All right, done." I could afford not to quibble; the money would come out of Peter Erskine's pocket eventually, not mine. I took two twenties and a ten from my wallet and laid them on the table between us, but I kept my hand on the bills when Lenihan reached for them. "After you've told me and I'm sure you're being straightforward."

"Hey," he said, and now he sounded wounded and put-upon, "one thing I don't do is lie for personal gain. Not even to my friends."

"Good for you. Who told you about Vok's vow of vengeance?"

"The nurse who was in the room at the time. Ellen Bowers."

"Why did she confide in you?"

"We hook up now and then, Ellen and me. She knows I'm into the world of weird and this Vok thing was right up my alley." A sly grin. "I showed her my appreciation with dinner and a good fuck."

My reaction to that was an expressionless stare, to let him know I was not going to play the see-what-a-stud-I-am-wink-wink game. "What did she have to say about the other man in the room? You didn't mention him in your blog piece."

"What other man?"

"Relative or friend of Vok's, apparently."

"Yeah? Well, I can't help you there. Ellen never mentioned anybody else being in the room."

"Sure about that?"

"Positive. I'd've put it into the write-up if she had."

"Did you ask her who claimed the bodies of Vok and his wife?"

"Nobody claimed them."

"Oh?"

"Ellen checked for me," Lenihan said. "No next of kin located and nobody else came forward. Both bodies planted at county expense."

I mulled that over for a few seconds before I asked, "Did you turn up any names in the Voks' apartment—other individuals who might be involved in this cult they belonged to?"

"Ah . . . I can't answer that."

"No? Why not?"

He looked a little sheepish now. "Well, the truth is, I went there, but the place was locked up tight and I couldn't convince the building manager to let me in."

"Then how did you find out about the books and the other black arts stuff the Voks had?"

"I didn't." The grin again, and a shrug. "Details make for a better story, whether they've been confirmed or not. Poetic license, you know?"

"Meaning you made up that part of it?"

"Well, not completely. The grimoires I listed are all genuine volumes, and I figured there were bound to be pentagrams and other shit linking the Voks to a devil cult."

Some journalist. "But you don't know that there was."

"No. But Vok admitted to Satan being his lord and master. Pact with the devil, right?"

"That doesn't mean it's true," I said. "He was dying, angry, probably not in his right mind."

"You're forgetting the black host. Ellen saw him shove it into the guy's hand. The wife nearly freaked when she saw it, so it must've been genuine. That and the vow makes Vok a devil worshipper in my book."

But not in mine, not necessarily. "Does Ellen Bowers still work at South Bay Memorial?"

"Yep."

"On duty today, would you know?"

He shook his head. "We're not that close."

"But you do have the hospital's phone number?"

"Sure. Ellen's, too, if you want it."

"Both."

"Do I get the fifty bucks then?"

I told him yes, and he said he'd have to get the numbers from his cell. He went away through the curtains, came back pretty soon with them scrawled on a piece of notepaper. When I took my hand off the bills, he made them disappear as if by a little magic trick of his own.

He grinned again. "Nice doing business with you," he said. "Hope you find what you're looking for."

I didn't answer him, or return his salute as I turned to leave. I may have to deal with people who have shoddy morals and ethics, and who think nothing of cavalierly adding to the mis-information on the Internet, but I don't have to be polite to them.

8

In the car I called South Bay Memorial to find out if Ellen Bowers was on duty today. She was, but currently assisting on a surgery and unavailable until after two o'clock. So I programmed the Voks' former address, 1936 Dillard Street, into the GPS and let the thing guide me down 101 into San Jose.

The address was in one of the poorer parts of the city, a mixed neighborhood with Hispanics dominating. The building was a somewhat run-down, six-unit apartment house flanked by a bodega on one side, another apartment building on the other. Cooking odors old and new clogged the air in the narrow foyer. Pasted above the name Rodriguez on the mailbox for apartment #1 was an old DYMO label with the word *Manager* on it. I pushed the bell, waited, pushed it again. Just as I was about to try for a third and last time, the intercom crackled and a voice said, "Yeah? What is it?" The crackling was so bad I barely understood the words, and couldn't tell if the voice was male or female.

I gave my name and said I was there on a business matter, but none of it got through to whoever was on the other end. There was some staticky chatter that I couldn't understand at all; another attempt on my part didn't get through, either. The intercom shut off, and a few seconds later the door to a ground-floor apartment popped open and a guy in an armless undershirt came out. He peered through the front door glass at me, yanked it open, and snapped irritably, "Goddamn thing don't never work right," as if the intercom's failings were my fault. "What you want? Selling something, we don't want it."

"I'm not a salesman. You're Mr. Rodriguez?"

"I asked you what you want."

"To talk to the manager. Is that you?"

"No, my wife, but she's at work." He didn't say why he wasn't also at work, but then maybe he had a night job. And a tolerant employer, if so, since he reeked of beer. "No empty units, if that's what you're looking for."

"It's not. What I'm looking for is some information on a couple who lived here over a year ago. The Voks—Antanas and Elza Vok."

"Them two." Rodriguez scowled at me. He was a big guy, forty or so, with hairy arms and chest and a hanging beer gut that hid the belt buckle on his trousers. "They're dead, killed in a car smash. Why you want to know about them?"

"I'm trying to locate their next of kin."

"Why? What for?"

"Can you help me, Mr. Rodriguez?"

"No. I mind my own business, man. Besides, them other guys was pretty damn creepy."

"What other guys?"

"The two come around here and took some of the Voks' stuff away."

"When was this? How soon after the car smash?"

"Morning after he died in the hospital."

Fast work, if Rodriguez's memory was accurate. The kind that suggests urgency and purpose.

"Can you describe the men?" I asked.

"After a year? Come on, man."

"I'd appreciate it if you'd try to remember."

He didn't have to try very hard; he remembered them, all right. Pretty soon he said, "One was like the Voks. You know, foreign."

"Lithuanian?"

A fat shoulder lifted, dropped again.

"What about the other one?"

"White guy. Butt ugly, built like an ox. They wasn't the painting brothers, that's for sure."

"Painting brothers?"

"Yeah. Sign on the door of the van they had."

"The Painting Brothers, that was the company name?"

"No, no. The brothers' name was the same as that guy used to be on late-night TV. The talk show guy."

"I don't watch late-night TV."

"Leno, man. *L-e-n-o.* Leno Brothers Painting."

"Do you recall where the business was located?"

"Nah. My memory ain't that good."

"How old would you say the two men were?"

"Not as old as the Voks. I didn't look at them too close. Creepy, like I said."

"In what way?"

"Just creepy," Rodriguez said. "You know how you meet somebody, strangers, you get these vibes tell you you don't want to have nothing to do with them? Like that."

"Were you the one who let them into the Voks' apartment?"

"Not me. My wife took 'em up."

"How did you and she know they were authorized to remove the Voks' belongings?"

"They had a paper."

"What kind of paper?"

Another shrug. "Maria was okay with it. Didn't think they was as creepy as I did . . . ain't nothing much bothers her. Anyway, why should we care? Sooner they got the stuff out, sooner we could rent the unit again. The owner don't like empty apartments."

"Did they take everything the Voks owned?"

"Left the furniture," Rodriguez said. "Clothes, too. Crappy stuff, all of it. We had to dump the clothes at Goodwill. But not the furniture—new renters didn't have none of their own, and they didn't care it was crappy."

"What exactly did the men haul away?"

"Cartons full of stuff. Took 'em a couple of hours."

"Any idea what was in the cartons?"

Shrug. "Don't know, don't care."

"Were you or your wife ever in the apartment when the Voks lived in it?"

"Hell, no. They didn't want nobody in there. Kept to themselves, never had much to say."

"Did they have many visitors?"

"Not that I seen. Never paid no attention." Rodriguez belched beerily and squinted down his nose at me. "Hey, all these questions. How come you want to know so much about the Voks?"

"I told you, I'm trying to track down their next of kin."

"Yeah, well, you come to the wrong place, man." He belched again. "I got no more time to talk. Things to do inside."

Like open another beer. "Thanks for your time, Mr. Rodriguez. *Buenas tardes.*"

"Yeah," he said, and backed up and shut the door in my face.

9

I looked up Leno Brothers Painting on my trusty new iPhone. Just about every business has a website these days, and this outfit was no exception. They were located in Campbell, a small city adjacent to San Jose on the west. The two brothers were Floyd and Harvey and there were photographs of each on the site; the one named Harvey appeared to qualify as "butt ugly, built like an ox." They evidently ran a cut-rate outfit with emphasis on speed rather than quality of work. "Nobody Beats Our Prices. Fastest Brushes in the West."

The address turned out to be in an industrial area not far off Highway 17. Narrow piece of property sandwiched between an outfit that sold solenoid valves and a plumbing supply company's pipe yard. The building's exterior was neither run-down nor prosperous looking—just a small, nondescript blue-collar business like thousands of others. A none too clean white van sat in the driveway alongside, facing the street.

An overhead bell rang a couple of off-key notes when I entered. The interior, unoccupied at the moment, wasn't much to look at, either. There was a linoleum-topped counter with some paint-sample books on it, a stack of gallon cans with a placard propped against them that had the words *Sale—Big Savings* written on it, and walls adorned with photographs of freshly painted houses by way of advertisement for the Leno brothers' handiwork.

Beyond the counter was an areaway that apparently led to a workroom and storage area at the rear. A man wearing a stained white smock and painters' cap appeared there and walked up to the counter, wiping his hands on a large rag, not quite hurrying. The Leno named Floyd—smaller, leaner, and older than his brother, craggy faced, eyes the shiny color of black olives. His forehead, under a thatch of thinning, dust-colored hair, was oddly crosshatched with a pattern of lines that resembled nothing so much as a tic-tac-toe drawing.

"Yes, sir? Help you?"

"Mr. Leno?"

"Floyd Leno, that's right."

Under normal circumstances I would have showed him ID and come straight to the point of my visit, as I'd done with Lenihan and Rodriguez. But these were not normal circumstances. So I played a role instead.

"I'm not here about a painting job or anything like that," I said, making my voice hesitant and a little nervous, as if I were unsure of myself. "I . . . well, I understand you knew a man named Vok."

"Who?"

"Vok. Antanas Vok."

You had to be paying close attention to see the change in his eyes, like shutters coming down over a pair of tiny windows. Otherwise his expression remained the same. "Name's not familiar. Customer of ours?"

"I don't think so, no. I thought he must be . . . well, a good friend of you and your brother."

"Why would you think that?"

"On account of your brother and another friend cleaned out the Voks' apartment after they were killed in that accident last year."

He looked at me steadily while he did some more hand-wiping; the rag smelled strongly of turpentine. "Who told you that?"

"Tenant in the building where they used to live."

"He made a mistake," Leno said. "I told you, I don't know anybody named Vok."

"But maybe your brother does. Is he here?"

"Out on a job. What's your interest in this Vok anyway?"

I cleared my throat before I said, "I met him where he used to work, not long before he was killed. We had a talk one night."

"Talk about what?"

"About this . . . group he belonged to."

"What kind of group?"

"People who believe in doing things other people wouldn't approve of. It sounded like something I'd like try, but I . . . I guess I wasn't ready at the time. And then there was the accident and Vok hadn't given me the names of anybody else in the group, so I tried to forget about it. But I couldn't. Things haven't been going too well for me lately, and now . . . well, I'm ready for a change, a new way of living the rest of my life."

"I don't know what you're talking about, mister."

"You sure? I mean, I'm serious about wanting to get into this group. Real serious. I've got a little money saved, if that's what it takes . . ."

Apparently it wasn't. "You're not making any sense," he said. There was a cold steel edge in his voice now. The black eyes no longer seemed shuttered; they were fixed on me in a glazed, unblinking stare, like that of a corpse. "And you're wasting my time; I got work to do. Go peddle your bullshit someplace else."

"It's not bullshit—"

"It is to me. You know what's good for you, mister, you won't come around here anymore. My brother's got even less patience than me, and a mean temper when he's bugged for no reason."

"Are you . . . threatening me?"

"Call it friendly advice," Leno said. He threw the smelly rag down on the counter, gestured at the door. "On your way."

Bust. Maybe I hadn't played the role well enough. Maybe Leno and his brother weren't involved in a devil cult after all. Maybe, if they were, the cult wasn't taking in new communicants. Or maybe in order to join you had to be sponsored by one of the members, to ensure complete secrecy.

Too many maybes. Unless Tamara could turn up something useful on the Leno brothers, what they amounted to was a dead end.

10

I don't like hospitals.

My antipathy isn't as strong as Jake Runyon's—he spent long months watching his second wife die of ovarian cancer in a Seattle hospital—but it's strong enough. I've been inside one or another too damn often, as patient and visitor both, the last time in Placerville on a two-day vigil after Kerry's kidnap ordeal, praying for her to pull out of a semi-coma. There's nothing worse than seeing someone you love hooked up to machines and IVs, dying or perilously close to it. No one who has gone through that can ever be comfortable in a hospital again, even on the kind of brief professional mission that took me to South Bay Memorial. I could feel myself tightening up, my pulse rate jump, as soon as I walked through the door into the main lobby. Health care facility. Right. The sooner I got this visit over with, the better *my* health care would be.

I told the woman staffing the Information Desk that I wanted to speak with Nurse Ellen Bowers on a personal matter. She checked a list, made a call, and then directed me to the nurses' station on the third floor. Two nurses up there, one of each sex; the woman wasn't Ellen Bowers. Ms. Bowers was "on her rounds," the male nurse told me, and expected back shortly.

There were some chairs in a small waiting area, one of which I was invited to occupy. So I sat there and did what I could to block out the hospital sounds and smells by ruminating on the Rodriguez and Floyd Leno interviews.

Harvey Leno and an unidentified Lithuanian, with a paper allegedly authorizing the removal of the Voks' personal belongings. Why in such a hurry? There could be an innocent cultural explanation, if the Lithuanian was a friend or close relative. It also could have something to do with the nature of those belongings, if Lenihan had been closer to the truth than he realized in his made-up description of the apartment's black arts–related contents. No way now that I could see, after the Leno blow-off, of finding out which.

I'd been waiting there seven or eight minutes when Ellen Bowers returned to the station. I hadn't let myself form any preconceived notions about what she'd be like, and it was just as well. There was nothing particularly memorable about her unless you were a man attracted to large-breasted women—Lenihan's preference, no doubt. Late thirties, wheat-blond hair, a little on the plump side. Large gray eyes, the irises rimmed in black—her best feature. A pleasantly quizzical smile took on a sardonic edge when I introduced myself and told her how I'd gotten her name.

"My good friend Joe," she said, as if he were anything but. "What did he tell you about me?"

"About you personally? Nothing." I was not about to repeat Lenihan's uncalled-for sexual comment. "Just that you were the source of an article he wrote for his blog about a year ago, concerning an accident victim named Antanas Vok."

"Oh . . . that. Is that why you're here? I thought maybe Joe told you I . . ." She didn't finish the sentence, but I had a pretty good idea what she'd been about to say. If Lenihan bragged about her as an easy score to others as casually as he had to a stranger like me, he was an even bigger schmuck than I'd taken him for.

"You were present when Vok delivered his vengeance threat, is that right?"

"Yes, I was there, and I wish to God I hadn't been. Is that why you're here? That unholy business?"

I said it was, and gave her a look at the license photostat.

She blinked at it. "Why would a private investigator be interested, after all this time? My God, don't tell me something's happened to . . . the person who was threatened?"

"No. Confidential matter, Ms. Bowers."

"You realize I can't tell you the person's name?"

"That isn't one of my questions. Do you mind talking about the incident?"

Several seconds ticked away. She seemed about to decline, then changed her mind. "I suppose not," she said. "But you'll have to make it brief. I have duties."

"As brief as I can. What Joe Lenihan wrote on his blog is essentially what happened that day?"

"*Exactly* what happened. I'm never likely to forget what that dreadful little man said and did before he died."

"The threat was just as Lenihan quoted it?"

"Word for word," Ms. Bowers said. "I have a very good memory. Too good in that case."

"Would you say Vok was in his right mind at the time?"

"Right mind? I doubt that man was ever in his right mind."

"So you don't think what he said had any sort of factual basis."

"Well, *he* believed every single word. Actually believed he'd made a pact with the devil. Oh, he was one of them, all right. You should have seen his face. His eyes . . . I swear they glowed like fire the whole time. Brrr. Gives me chills just thinking about it."

"You witnessed him passing the black host?"

"That little black disc? Yes. Vok grabbed the man's arm and pushed the thing into his hand."

"Where did he get it, do you know?"

"It must've been in his shoe."

"Shoe?"

"As weak and near death as he was that morning," Ms. Bowers said, "he kept asking for his shoe, the right shoe. Doctor Adamson, the attending physician, said it couldn't hurt to grant the request if the shoes hadn't been disposed of in the ER cleanup. They hadn't been, and I brought the right one up."

"Was it Doctor Adamson who telephoned . . . let's call him the victim?"

"Yes. The phone call was Vok's first demand; he made it over and over until the doctor agreed. Dying patients' final requests, no matter how strange, are honored whenever possible."

"What was the victim's reaction to the black host?"

"No reaction, he just stared at it. But his wife . . . she gasped and turned white as a sheet, I thought she was going to faint when Vok started babbling about Satan."

"Did either of them say anything to him?"

"No."

"Or he say anything more to them?"

"Not a word. The victim shoved the thing into his pocket,

grabbed his wife's arm, and hurried her out of there. Vok flat-lined less than two minutes after they were gone."

"What about the other man in the room? What can you tell me about him?"

". . . I'm sorry?"

"The other man, the one who evidently came to visit Vok."

"I don't know who you mean," Ms. Bowers said. "As far as I'm aware, the patient had no other visitors at all."

"There was no one else in the room at the time?"

"Just the victim and his wife, Vok, and myself. Did Joe tell you there was?"

"No."

"Well, whoever did was mistaken or misinformed."

No, I thought, the individual was making it up. And why would Peter Erskine tell me such a dead-bang lie?

11

The main ingredients in detective work are the gathering and interpretation of facts, plus a certain amount of legwork. But instinct also plays a role when you've been at it long enough, a kind of sixth sense that generally comes into play in one of two instances: when an investigation is proceeding well and nearing conclusion, or when the facts indicate you've unintentionally gone or deliberately been led astray. In the latter case, the intuitive feeling is sharp and grows sharper the more attention you pay to it.

Something was wrong here. The kind of wrongness that smacks of manipulation and deceit.

I sat ruminating in the hospital parking lot for the better part of ten minutes. The thinking produced a couple of notions, neither of which I liked worth a damn. Follow-up time. I programmed Erskine's office address into the GPS and pointed the car north.

The address was just off El Camino Real in downtown Menlo Park, a few miles from the Erskines' Atherton home— an older, modernized building that housed three attorneys, an architectural firm, and an orthodontist in addition to Peter

Erskine, Financial Advisor. His business name was displayed in fancy gilt script on the frosted glass door. I opened it and went on in.

The woman working on a computer at one of two desks jumped a little at my entrance, as if startled at the appearance of a visitor. She blinked, saw that I was no one she knew, and blinked some more. The professional smile that finally beamed on had a little twitch at one corner.

"Oh, I'm sorry," she said as I shut the door. "I wasn't expecting anyone. May I help you?"

"I'd like a few words with Mr. Erskine."

"I'm sorry," she said again. "He's not here. He left half an hour ago. Did you have an appointment?"

"No appointment. Do you expect him back this afternoon?"

"No, I'm sorry"—for the third time—"not until tomorrow."

"Would you happen to know where he went?"

"I really couldn't say. What was it you wanted to see him about?"

I didn't answer immediately. The anteroom was large and on the posh side, as befitted the type of business Erskine was in: thick carpeting, neatly arranged chrome-and-leather furniture, blandly tasteful prints on the walls. But it had an unused look about it, as if the office were newly opened instead of well established. The young woman's desk contained a blotter, a telephone, and the computer she'd been using; the unoccupied desk had nothing at all on it except a covered computer terminal. One of two closed doors at the rear bore Erskine's name; the second was unmarked.

Except for the twitchy smile, the woman fit well into the

posh surroundings. No older than twenty-five, and decora-
tively attractive in the characterless fashion of so many young
people these days: small of stature, shoulder-length hair a thick
glossy black, green eyes large, luminous, and canny in an un-
sophisticated way. Judging from as much as I could see of her
body behind the desk, she was eye candy in that respect, too.

"Sir? What was it you wanted to see Mr. Erskine about?"

"Private business matter."

"I see. Well, if you'd like to leave a message or a number
where he can reach you . . ."

"No, thanks, I'll try him at his home. You're Melanie Vinson, is that right?"

"How did you—" The corner of her mouth twitched again.
"Did Mr. Erskine tell you my name?"

"Is there a reason he shouldn't have?"

"No." Twitch. "No, of course not."

"Must be an interesting job, working with a stockbroker."

"Yes, it is. Very. And very demanding." Twitch. "Well. If
you're sure you don't want to leave a message for Mr. Erskine,
I have quite a bit of work to do before I leave for the day."

"I won't keep you from it, then."

I turned for the door, but before I reached it she said, "Um,
in case you don't connect with Mr. Erskine at his home, whom
should I say stopped in to see him?"

I gave her my name. It was not the first time she'd heard it
in this office; the smile twitched all the way off and sharp little
teeth nibbled at her lower lip before she dropped her gaze to
the computer keyboard and began typing. Not good at hiding
her emotions, the nervous Ms. Vinson.

Why would a man with Peter Erskine's bizarre problem
confide to his secretary/assistant that he'd hired a private

234 • Bill Pronzini

investigator? One more question that needed answering, and honed even more the sense of manipulation and deceit I felt.

The tall wrought-iron gates were closed across the foot of the Erskines' entrance drive. Locked, too; I got out of the car and tried them. There was an intercom device on one of the pillars. I pushed the pearl button below the speaker, waited, got no response, and tried twice more with the same lack of results. Nobody home. Or nobody home who wanted to be disturbed by a caller no matter who he happened to be.

Before driving away I hauled out the iPhone and called the agency and asked Tamara to do a deeper background check on Peter Erskine. Emphasis on his business practices and personal finances.

"How come?" she asked.

"He lied to me, that's how come, and I haven't been able to find him to ask why." I told her what I'd learned from Ellen Bowers. "No reason for the lie that I can see unless he's got some sort of hidden agenda."

"Such as?"

"I'm not sure yet. That's why I need more data on him, his marriage, his personal life, his business activities. Anything you can dig up that'll give me a better handle on the man."

"Right."

"And while you're at it, run a check on his assistant, Melanie Vinson."

"Ah hah," she said. "So you do think she might be more to him than just office help."

"Could be. She was a lot less professional today than a woman in her position ought to be. She's got something on her mind that doesn't involve stocks and bonds."

"I'll get right on it."

"One more search you can run for me when you have the time. Floyd and Harvey Leno, *L-e-n-o,* owners of Leno Brothers Painting in Campbell."

"Who're they?"

"Devil cultists . . . maybe. One of them helped clear out the Voks' apartment the day after he died. I had a little talk with Floyd Leno this afternoon. Nonproductive, but provocative."

"So you want the full package on them, too?"

"Right. Whatever seems relevant."

"Okay. You coming back to the city now?"

"On my way. Not the office, though—home."

"I'll get back to you ASAP."

"It can all wait until tomorrow. Why don't you give yourself a break, go home early for a change?"

"I *am* home," she said, "right here at my desk. That place on Potrero Hill I pay too much rent for is just where I go to sleep."

12

Rush-hour traffic heading into the city and on the way up to Diamond Heights added twenty-some minutes to my travel time from Atherton. It was nearly six when I walked into the condo. I'd been there all of five minutes, just enough time to say hello to Emily—Kerry was still at Bates and Carpenter—and open a beer from the fridge when Tamara called.

She'd already run all the backgrounders I'd asked for and compiled fairly substantial dossiers on Peter Erskine, Melanie Vinson, and the Leno brothers. It never takes her long to gather even the most obscure data available on any individual within radar range.

"First off," she said, "the Erskines' marriage isn't so solid after all. Turns out she filed for divorce two and a half years ago, but they reconciled before it ever got to court."

"What prompted the divorce action?"

"Not specified, but I picked up some hints he was having himself a fling and she found out about it."

"You get the woman's name?"

"No. Hush-hush on that. But it probably wasn't Melanie

Vinson. She didn't start working for Erskine until sixteen months ago."

"So he strayed at least once."

"At least."

"And his wife won't stand for it happening again. Likely the reconciliation was based on his promise to walk the line and a threat to go through with the divorce if she caught him a second time."

"Right. If she caught him. Doesn't mean he's been Mr. Faithful since, just extracareful."

I said musingly, "Marian Erskine's no dummy, and with all her money she figures to have sound legal representation. Two failed marriages and the third a trophy husband spells prenup to me."

"Did to me, too. There was one, I found out that much, but of course I couldn't get the details."

"Usual kind of arrangement, probably. Settlement for X amount of dollars in the event of divorce, with no claim on anything she owned prior to the marriage. I assume that includes the Atherton property?"

"Does. She inherited that along with her pop's millions."

"What about Erskine's personal finances?"

"Well, he's a lousy stockbroker," Tamara said. "Lost bundles in the market on dubious investments, his own money as well as his clients'. One of the clients threatened him with a lawsuit for fraud. Most of the others quit him quick. He's only got a couple left, just barely hanging on."

"And I take it his wife won't bail him out."

"Did at first, then apparently got tired of the money drain and shut it off. Letting him sink or swim on his own, and he's going down fast."

"I figured as much," I said. "Didn't look as though much if anything was going on in that office of his. The Vinson woman seemed surprised to have somebody walk in unexpectedly."

"Keeps it open and her on salary for appearance sake. Either that, or because he's banging her."

"Uh-huh. Anything more on him I should know?"

"Nothing relevant. Unless the fact that he doesn't drink means something. Won't touch any kind of alcohol, makes a big deal out of it, evidently. My body's my temple kind of thing."

"Either that," I said, "or it's a matter of self-discipline. He's the type who doesn't like to lose control."

"Must not like being under his wife's thumb, then. Seems she calls all the shots in the marriage."

"Yes, it does."

"Okay. Melanie Vinson. Erskine didn't hire her because of her stock market savvy or secretarial skills. She didn't have either. Before she went to work for him, she was a saleswoman in a Palo Alto boutique. And before that, a student at San Jose State."

"Any idea whether she met Erskine by applying for the job, or he offered it to her after they met some other way?"

"Nope. Want to bet it was after they met? Party, club, someplace like that."

"No bet."

"Here's the rest of what I pulled up on her," Tamara said. "Born in San Diego, family moved to Milpitas when she was twelve. Father deceased, mother still living. No siblings. Never married. Drama major at S.J.S., wanted to be an actress like about twenty million other kids her age. Small parts in two school plays. Dropped out after a year and a half—lack of funds. Family set up a college fund for her when she was little, but it wasn't substantial enough to carry her through. She wasn't doing well anyway. Not enough talent or ambition and likely poor study habits."

"Any sort of police record?"

"Arrested once for shoplifting a bottle of perfume when she was eighteen. That's all."

"Where does she live?"

"Palo Alto. Expensive apartment building. And her ride is a BMW Z4 sports car. Even secondhand, those babies don't come cheap, and she's had it less than a year." Tamara chuckled and said sardonically, "Erskine must be paying her a pretty hefty salary for sitting around that half-dead office of his. I wonder why."

What she'd turned up on the Leno brothers was not particularly illuminating. Harvey Leno had a minor record— arrested twice, once for public drunkenness, once for aggravated assault, both more than a dozen years past. Married briefly and divorced in the late nineties, no children, no living relatives other than his brother. Floyd Leno was a bachelor with no brushes with the law of any kind. More or less model citizens, on the surface. Paid their bills and taxes on time, made a modest but steady living out of their painting company. Not a whisper of any trafficking with Satanists or other illegal or dubious activities.

Definite dead end there. If I continued my investigation, I would need to scrounge up another lead. If I continued it. The way things were shaping up now, I was pretty sure I wouldn't.

After Tamara and I rang off, I went out onto the balcony—it

was a warmish night, clear, myriad lights twinkling in the city panorama spread out below—to do some hard thinking.

So Peter Erskine was a business failure with financial troubles and a sick wife who held tight to the purse strings and kept him on a short leash. What I'd have liked to know were the terms of her will, whether or not he stood to inherit all or some of her fortune if she predeceased him. But as with the conditions of their prenup, there was no legal way to find out. Except from her, in answer to a direct question—an unlikely prospect.

The more I thought the more convinced I was that Erskine had a hidden agenda of the nastiest sort. The facts Tamara and I had come up with, the inferences to be drawn from them and from the lies he'd told me, all pointed to it. Some of the details were hazy yet, but the overall design was clear enough. Vengeance vows, Satanic covenants, black masses and black hosts, evil spirits in human form . . . none of that mattered anymore if I was right.

But it was all just speculation at this point, without a foundation of proof to support it. If I went to the police with uncorroborated suspicions about a bizarre plot with supernatural overtones, I'd come across as a head case in spite of my longstanding reputation as a reliable investigator.

The only other way to proceed was problematic. I'm always leery of stepping into a volatile situation without hard evidence, but in this case, where it might well mean saving a woman's life, it was my moral duty to run the risk. And do it quick. But I had to be careful. Very careful. Sticking my oar in could backfire on me and on the agency—leave us wide open to legal action for harassment and defamation of character.

We'd been on the receiving end of a similar kind of lawsuit once before, unjustly and maliciously, and if it hadn't been for the plaintiff's sudden demise before the case went to court the judgment could have gone against us and put us out of business.

All right, then. Tomorrow I would find a way to have a private face-to-face with Marian Erskine, then another with her husband.

I did not have those face-to-face meetings. By then it was too late—too damn late.

Marian Erskine was already dead, of a massive heart attack suffered at her home that same night.

13

It was Tamara who gave me the news when I came into the agency in the morning. She'd decided to see if she could pull up anything more on the Erskines, and there it was. Nothing happens of any newsworthy interest in this world today that isn't reported and disseminated almost immediately on the Internet, and Marian Erskine had been a prominent figure in the Atherton community as well as a major contributor to charitable causes. One more example of the two-edged sword of modern technology: good for business purposes, disastrous for privacy.

People with weak hearts die suddenly all the time. The fatal attacks don't have to be induced by external means, and even when they are there is no way to prove it without witnesses and/or some sort of physical evidence. Marian Erskine had reportedly been alone when she suffered her coronary, her "bereaved" husband away at a business dinner in Palo Alto. She hadn't died at the Atherton home; she'd been found on the rear terrace alive and unconscious—by none other than Melanie Vinson, who'd made the 911 call—and taken to Peninsula General Hospital, where she succumbed at 10:06 P.M. Tragic death by natural causes.

I didn't believe it.

Marian Erskine had been murdered. Cleverly and cold-bloodedly, with malice aforethought.

I said as much to Tamara. And to Jake Runyon, who had arrived a few minutes before I did and been briefed on the situation.

Tamara said, "So you figure the whole thing was a setup by Erskine to scare his wife into a fatal attack."

"Everything except Vok's shenanigans in the hospital; the revenge vow was genuine enough. Erskine built his plan on that, hatched it after she had her first coronary and barely survived. She might've had another attack as suddenly as the first, but she might also have lived for years. Seems pretty obvious he married her for her money and that he didn't want to wait any longer to gain control of it."

"Assuming she made him beneficiary in her will and didn't write him out after she caught him cheating."

"Sole or major beneficiary, right," I said. "Has to be that way. As far as the plan goes, her credulous belief in the supernatural made it easy for him. A little research was all he needed to manufacture an imitation black host, create the rest of the revenant illusion. I'd be willing to bet he encouraged her cognac drinking, too, whenever the two of them were alone—to weaken her heart even more. Then it was just a matter of escalating the threat. Whatever he arranged to happen last night terrified her enough to do the job."

"Adds up that way for me, too. Jake?"

Runyon nodded his agreement. He's a good man and a good detective, formerly with the Seattle PD and one of the Pacific Northwest's larger private security firms before he went to work for us. He'd moved to San Francisco after his second wife's cancer death, to try to reconcile with his estranged son by his first wife, but the reconciliation hadn't worked out. His way of dealing with lingering grief and loneliness was to throw himself into his work; he put in more hours on the job than even Tamara did.

"But there's one thing I don't get," she said. "Why did Erskine want to hire a detective?"

I said, "I don't think he did."

"You mean it was his wife's idea?"

"That's right. Dominant decision maker, holder of the purse strings—she'd have insisted on it to try to disprove the supernatural explanation. He couldn't talk her out of it without arousing her suspicions, so he pretended it was his idea. And tried his lying best to misdirect me, keep me focused on Vok's alleged connection to a devil cult."

"Who'd he have helping him, impersonating Vok? Vinson's the one who made the nine-one-one call."

"What did the report say she was doing at the Erskine house at that time of night?"

"Delivering some business papers."

"Pretty thin excuse, given that his business is in the dumper."

"Yeah, but she still tried to save Mrs. Erskine's life with the nine-one-one call."

"Maybe not," Runyon said. "Maybe she was supposed to make sure the woman was dead before making the call and misdiagnosed. Even doctors get fooled sometimes."

"So then she could be in it with Erskine. She does the dirty work while he's off establishing an alibi for himself, just in case."

A clutch of frustrated anger made me say, "Dammit, I

should have put this together sooner. Gone down there to see her last night instead of waiting. I might have been able to forestall what happened, convince her she was the real target."

Runyon said, "And you might not have been able to do either. Don't blame yourself. You were on the case less than two days—that's little enough time to wade through misdirection and subterfuge." The calm voice of reason, as usual with him.

"It's still galling. I hate like hell being used."

"Don't we all."

"What bites my ass," Tamara said, "is that Erskine's probably gonna get away with it."

I said, "Not if I have anything to say about it. There has to be a way to expose him."

"What way? There's no proof."

"None yet. Doesn't mean we can't find some."

"How?"

"You could try rattling his cage a little," Runyon said. "Let him know you're on to him, see if you can get him to self-incriminate."

"Pretty difficult to manage if I'm reading him right," I said. "But it'll do for starters."

I rang up the Erskine home. No answer. Peter Erskine's cell number next. Straight to voice mail. The message I left made no mention of his wife's death; let him think I hadn't heard about it yet. I said I had uncovered some information about Antanas Vok that he should know about and requested a call-back ASAP. If he was checking his messages today, it shouldn't be too long before I heard from him.

An idea occurred to me—a long shot but worth taking

a chance on. I went into Tamara's office, asked her to find out which fire department's emergency response team had answered Melanie Vinson's 911 call. And if possible, the name or names of the individuals manning the EMT units, as well as the names of the ER doctors at Peninsula General who'd attended to Marian Erskine.

Tall order, and only partially successful. No luck on ID-ing the ER doctors. But it was the Menlo Park Fire Protection District that served Atherton and its Station 4 had responded with an Advanced Life Support engine manned by a fireman and a licensed paramedic. Their names were also unavailable, but I ought to be able to find that out by a visit to Station 4.

It was past noon, and the office routine was wearing on me, when Peter Erskine returned my call. He said in slow, sepulchral tones, "I'm afraid I have terrible news. My wife passed away last night. Her poor heart finally gave out."

"Yes," I said, "I just heard. My condolences."

"Thank you. It wasn't unexpected—she had a severe coronary three months ago—but I'm still in shock."

"Sure you are. She was alone at the time, I understand."

"Yes, and I blame myself for that. I had a business dinner scheduled in Palo Alto and Marian insisted I go. She said she'd be all right, she'd keep a pistol close at hand in case that Vok crazy showed up again."

"Did he?"

"I don't know. How would I know? There was no sign of anyone on the grounds." Erskine sighed heavily. "I wish to God I'd stayed home. I may have been able to save her if I'd been there when it happened."

"Or if your assistant had gotten there a little sooner."

"Yes. It was too late by then. Neither the paramedics nor the hospital ER doctors could do anything to revive her."

"How did Ms. Vinson happen to come to your home?"

"Miscommunication between us," Erskine said. "She brought some documents she'd been working on, thinking I needed them right away and that I'd be home. I completely forgot to tell her about the business dinner."

I said, "Why did she go around to the back terrace? That's where she found your wife, isn't it?"

"All the lights were on and there was no answer to the bell. My dear Marian was just lying there."

My dear Marian. Jesus. "And Ms. Vinson assumed she was already dead."

"She couldn't find a pulse and Marian didn't seem to be breathing."

"Big mistake on her part."

"Mistake?" Pause. "No, I can't fault her for that. She's had no medical training, doesn't know CPR."

"How come the gates were open, if she wasn't expected?"

". . . The gates?"

"She couldn't have driven onto the property otherwise. They open by remote control, so they must've been unlocked."

Longer pause this time, while he manufactured an answer. "You're right, of course," he said when he had one. "I must have released the lock button too soon after I drove out."

"I'd have thought you'd be more careful, under the circumstances."

"I should've been, yes. But locked gates didn't prevent that Vok lunatic from getting onto the property before."

"So it's a good possibility he did show up again last night. That he was the cause of your wife's attack."

"I suppose that's possible. But I'm the one he's after."

"Maybe he changed his tactics. Went after her instead."

"Why would he do that?"

"Could be she was a target, too. All along."

"I don't believe that." Stiffly, warily now. "No."

"In any case," I said, "another of those sudden appearances would have terrified her. And we both know how effective a weapon fear can be. As powerful and deadly a weapon as a gun or a knife."

No response for several beats. Then, "But we don't know he came again last night, do we."

"Did your wife have the pistol in her possession when Ms. Vinson found her?"

"The pistol? No, it was on the table near where she fell."

"Fired?"

"No." Pause. "You've kept all that Marian and I told you about Vok and the devil worshippers in confidence, haven't you?"

"Of course. You didn't tell the authorities about it, either, I take it."

"Hardly. This is a painful enough time for me. If the media got hold of that crazy business . . . well, you understand."

"All too well," I said.

Erskine made a tight little throat-clearing sound. "Why did you call me? Something to do with your investigation?"

"That's right. I picked up a pretty good lead. A couple of strangers showed up and cleaned out the Voks' apartment the morning after Vok died. Creepy types, according to the building manager."

"Members of that damned devil cult."

"If there is a devil cult."

"There has to be. Did you get their names?"

"Not yet. You want me to keep working on it?"

He was ready for that one. "Certainly. Why wouldn't I? As far as I know my life is still in danger."

"Sure it is." Clever bastard, all right. Keep up the pretense a while longer, let me run around chasing devil cultists that had nothing to do with him, then find a way to ease me out of the picture.

"I can't talk anymore right now," he said. "I'm due at the funeral home to make burial arrangements."

"One thing before you go. Whose decision was it to hire a detective, yours or your wife's?"

"What? Why do you want to know that?"

"Required for our files. Yours or your wife's?"

"Mine," Erskine said, and immediately broke the connection.

Okay. So I'd rattled his cage as much as I thought was wise at this point. He was perceptive as well as cunning; he'd gotten the message that I was on to him. It wouldn't worry him much right now—he was too sure of himself and the invincibility of his plan—but it might make him a little more vulnerable next time I talked to him. I would not be nearly as subtle when I did.

Still, my gut feeling was that it would take a lot more than words to break Peter Erskine. If he could be broken at all.

14

Menlo Park Fire Station 4 was a small building that housed a modern pumper and the Advanced Life Support vehicle. Originally it must have been solid brick, in keeping with its attractive upscale surroundings, but like so many brick structures that had survived the devastating Loma Prieta earthquake in '89, it had been redesigned and rebuilt to conform to seismic safety regulations. According to Tamara's search, it was manned 24/7 by a captain and two firefighters working shifts of seventy-two hours on, seventy-two hours off, and the trio working today were the same three who'd been on duty last night.

My investigator's license and mention of the fact that I was employed by Peter Erskine got me an audience with the captain. He was a little leery of me at first, until I assured him that I was not there to question his team's response time and lifesaving efforts; everybody these days, especially public servants, is litigation fearful and prickly because of it. Mr. Erskine, I explained, was only interested in knowing if his wife had been conscious at any time while she was being stabilized and/or during her transport to Peninsula General, and if so, if she'd said anything—any last words that might be a comfort to him. I don't like lying to people, particularly lies of this sort, but you do what you have to do in the interest of justice.

The captain didn't seem to find the request unusual. He said Mrs. Erskine had been conscious briefly, but couldn't tell me if she'd spoken. That information would have to come from the other two members of the team, and they were currently out on a call. I was welcome to wait for their return.

The wait lasted nearly an hour and a half. When the ALS unit finally pulled in, I had to hang on another fifteen minutes while they did some cleanup work on the engine. It was four o'clock by then. If the two firefighters had nothing to tell me, I'd head over to Peninsula General. The evening-shift ER personnel would have come on duty and I might be able to convince a doctor or nurse who had attended Marian Erskine to talk to me.

But it didn't come to that. The firefighters were cooperative, and the licensed paramedic, a young, linebacker-size Latino named Tejada, told me what I wanted to know.

"The woman was conscious, yes," he said, "but only for a minute or so as I was stabilizing her. She was in very bad shape. Frankly I was surprised she survived the ride to the hospital."

"Did she say anything?"

"Yes, but it didn't make too much sense."

"To me, either," the other firefighter said. He was an older man, a red-haired Irishman named Reilly. "Delirious mumblings."

"Can either of you recall what it was she said?"

"Something about shooting somebody, wasn't it, Alex?"

Tejada dipped his chin. "Sounded like 'I shot him three times but he wouldn't fall down; he just kept coming at me.'"

I made an effort to keep my expression blank so they couldn't tell how much significance those words held for me. "Is that all?"

"All that was coherent."

"Was there a gun anywhere near her when you got there?"

"A gun? No."

"Could one have been on a nearby table, maybe?"

Reilly said, "No gun. We'd've seen it if there was, after what she said about shooting somebody."

I thanked them and was about to leave when Tejada said, "You know, I just remembered something else she said. One word, just before she went under for good."

"What word?"

"*Reverend.*"

"Sure that's what it was?"

"Pretty sure." He shook his head sadly and crossed himself. "Knew she was dying, poor lady. Asking for a padre."

No, I thought as I went out to the car, she hadn't been asking for a padre. Tejada had misheard: the last word spoken by Marian Erskine hadn't been *reverend*.

It had been *revenant*.

So now I had a pretty good idea of how they'd worked it last night. Manufacture enough raw terror with the right kind of supernatural trappings and you can practically guarantee a weak heart will stop beating without ever laying a hand on the victim. Neat, clean, sadistically bloodless—the so-called perfect crime.

Like hell it was.

Prod Erskine some more now? I decided against it. Marian Erskine's last words were a piece of evidence against him, but only a small piece. Push him too far too soon, even if I made no direct accusation, and he was liable to sic a lawyer on me.

Better idea: he was the strong link, so go after the potential weak link instead.

Melanie Vinson.

If my take on her was accurate, she was a long way from being a mental giant—an easily manipulated follower who'd gone along with the murder scheme out of greed or love or a combination of both. In over her head, and at least a little scared; her twitchiness yesterday in Erskine's office, on the eve of her part in delivering the deathblow, suggested that.

Fear can be a weapon in serving justice, too, if you use it effectively. Turn hers back on her and it might well crack her wide open. And if she cracked, the odds were good she'd take Erskine down to save herself.

15

The offices of Peter Erskine, Financial Advisor were locked up tight. I hadn't expected otherwise, but the building was on my way out of Menlo Park and I had nothing to lose but a few minutes by stopping there first. I programmed Melanie Vinson's home address into the GPS, followed the disembodied voice's directions into Palo Alto and through a maze of residential streets not far from the Stanford University campus.

It was after five o'clock and already dark when the voice told me I'd arrived at my destination—a block of facing rows of town-house-style apartments extending back from the street in the shape of a broad horseshoe. Not a new complex, but well maintained, in a neighborhood so thick with shade trees it had a bucolic atmosphere. I'd seen modern rent/lease places like this before, often enough to know that there would be a courtyard with a communal swimming pool and recreation area in the middle of the two wings. Driveways angled up adjacent to each wing, along which were shedlike structures where the tenants parked their cars.

I wedged mine into a spot at the curb across the street. Before I got out, I transferred the voice-activated tape recorder

I keep in the glove compartment into my coat pocket. The night was clouding up and a cold wind had begun to blow; I pulled up the collar on my suit coat as I followed a walkway into an open foyer in the front curve of the horseshoe. Melanie Vinson occupied apartment #11; I rang the bell—once, twice, three times, leaning on it the last two. No response. Not home or ducking visitors if she was.

Thanks to Tamara, I had Vinson's landline and cell numbers written down in my notebook. Landline first: four rings, and an answering machine with one of those smart-ass-cute "you know what to do at the beep" messages kicked in. I clicked off before the beep sounded and tried the cell number: straight to voice mail.

Damn. Now what?

I went back outside. Crosswise paths led to the driveways along both sides. On impulse I followed the one that hooked around to the right, where the parking space for Vinson's apartment would be. Night-lights shone brightly back there, both inside and outside the covered parking structure. Each slant-in space had a unit number spray-painted on the tarmac. And tucked into #11 was a sleek black BMW Z4 sports car with a personalized license plate: MELSBBY. Mel's Baby. Mel for Melanie.

So either she was home and avoiding calls and callers or, more likely, she'd gone off with somebody. Erskine, probably. They had to be feeling good about the way the plan had gone, considering themselves inviolate despite my suspicions. Why not get together and celebrate the successful elimination of the woman who'd stood in the way of their lust for wealth, the sick woman who'd never done either of them any harm?

There was nobody in the parking area. I made sure of that,

then moved in alongside the BMW to the driver's door. Locked—naturally. I bent to peer through the window, but the overhead light was not strong enough to give me a clear look inside. About all I could make out was that neither of the bucket seats had anything on them.

I straightened up. More than a few people have a tendency to lose or misplace their car keys, or leave them in the ignition and then snap-lock the door when they get out, and as a safeguard some hide a spare key inside one of those little magnetized cases somewhere on the vehicle. If Melanie Vinson was one of them . . .

I eased around the front of the BMW, bending low to run my fingers behind the license plate and then along the underside of the bumper from one end to the other. All I felt was grit. I'd just started on the frame beneath the front fender and driver's side door panels when headlights splashed in along the driveway from the street.

I dropped to one knee and stayed there, in close to the car. Neither the beams nor the incoming vehicle reached as far as the #11 space; they angled into one closer to the street and immediately went dark. A man and a woman got out, chattering to each other, and drifted away toward a side entrance to the building wing. I didn't raise up until I heard a door slam over there.

There was nothing along the BMW's underbelly on this side, nothing under or inside the rear bumper. But then I got lucky. My fingers touched metal, felt the little square shape clipped up inside the rear wheel well on the passenger side.

I tugged the case loose. The spare key was inside. I fished it out, replaced the case where I'd found it. The spare had a couple of remote buttons on it, but I wasn't familiar with this make and model and had no idea if the remote made beeping sounds when you used it; some vehicles of this vintage operated that way. So I unlocked the driver's door with the key.

Quickly I wedged myself in under the wheel to cut off the interior light. Tight fit—I had a lot of pounds and girth on Melanie Vinson—but I could maneuver all right without adjusting the seat control.

The console storage compartment was locked, but the spare key opened that, too. I used my pencil flash to fast-check the contents. Registration slip, insurance card, half full package of menthol coffin nails, unopened packets of Kleenex and tampons . . . nothing to hold my attention. The slender pockets in both doors were empty. I squeezed out again, levered the driver's seat forward so I could look behind it and the one on the passenger side. The only items on the floor were a couple of empty Starbucks coffee containers and some wadded-up tissues.

I pushed the seat back in place, located and freed the trunk release before shutting the door. Around to the rear, then, to lift the trunk lid.

There was one item on the carpeted floor inside: a large, bulky laundry sack closed at the top by a drawstring. I loosened the string, widened the opening to see what was inside the bag.

Antanas Vok was inside the bag.

Shabby, ripped, dirt-caked black suit that stank of rotting meat. Stained white shirt. Old, dirty black shoes. Wide-brimmed black slouch hat. Realistic theatrical mask with dark bushy eyebrows and Vandyke beard glued on, the malleable latex material coated with some sort of luminous paint to give it an eerie glow in the dark. A pair of black gloves, fingers and thumbs on each painted to resemble skeletal hands.

There was a handgun, too, a .32-caliber Smith & Wesson five-shot revolver. I picked it up by the trigger guard, using the back of my index finger, and sniffed the barrel. Fired recently. With a couple of knuckles I broke the weapon to peer at the chambers. Three empty shells, two loaded ones. And all of them would be blanks. *I shot him three times, but he wouldn't fall down; he just kept coming at me.* Yeah, blanks.

No surprises in any of this. Vinson had to have been the one impersonating Vok; Erskine was too smart to bring a third party into the scheme. She was the right height, the same approximate size. With that outfit and the mask on, and the hat pulled down low over her forehead, she'd have passed easily for a middle-aged man. Plus she'd had acting experience, enough to pull off the menacing act with Erskine's help and guidance.

I stuffed everything back into the sack, retightened the drawstring, then lifted the bag out. I couldn't risk leaving it here without constant surveillance on the BMW; she might decide, or Erskine might tell her, to make it all disappear. I closed the trunk, relocked the driver's door, and pocketed the key in case it became necessary to return the sack at some point. Then I swung it up over my shoulder and quick-stepped down the empty driveway.

Two cars passed on my way to where I'd parked mine, but so far as I could tell none of the occupants paid any attention to me. Tenants hauling their laundry to a nearby Laundromat were common sights in almost any neighborhood. Just the same, I felt an easing of tension once the bag was locked away in the trunk.

. . .

What had taken place at the Erskine home last night was clear now. It must have gone something like this:

In costume Vinson slips onto the property same as the other times, catches Marian Erskine unaware inside the house or already sitting out on the terrace, advances on her in a threatening manner. Victim has the gun in hand or close to hand, fires three of what she believes are live rounds. Vinson keeps coming, the way a genuine revenant would. And in horror and sudden savage pain down goes Marian Erskine.

Then Vinson makes her first mistake. She's supposed to be certain the victim is dead before calling 911, but haste and nervousness cause her to misdiagnose; she doesn't realize until the firefighters arrive that Mrs. Erskine is still alive. Bad moment for her, but she manages to hang on to her nerve. By then she's retrieved the gun, gone to wherever she stashed her regular clothing, changed, loaded the costume and weapon into the laundry bag, and hid the bag in the trunk of her car.

Her second mistake was leaving the bag there. Maybe she was supposed to get rid of the contents somewhere, or at least hide the revolver inside her apartment until she could return it to Erskine. Or maybe she just didn't think there was any hurry. From her perspective, no one had any reason to search her car.

I had a case now against the two of them: my testimony, Marian Erskine's dying words, the array of sure to be fingerprint-laden evidence in the sack. But it was by no means conclusive, not where a wealthy Atherton citizen and allegedly bereaved widower was concerned. Enough, maybe, to convince the local authorities to mount an investigation, but just as likely not. I needed more solid proof.

So?

Couple of options. Pack it in for the day, go home to my family, and take steps tomorrow to see Melanie Vinson alone and try to crack her as I'd originally intended. Or stay put for a while in the hope that she'd return at a reasonable hour and I could brace her tonight. If she was with Erskine and he went into her town house with her, all the better. I liked the prospect of bracing the two of them together in a place he had no good reason for being the day after his wife's death, catching them off guard, making an effort to provoke her if not him into an incriminating slip with the tape recorder running. I'd settle for Vinson alone, but it was Erskine I most wanted to confront.

The second option, then. I dislike stakeouts after sitting through scores of them over the years, but I was angry and determined enough to tolerate one more of short duration. And I had a good vantage point from here, a clear look at the front entrance to the complex. Seven-thirty now. Give it a couple of hours at least.

I called Kerry to tell her I'd be home late, then tried to make myself comfortable. Good luck with that, in Tamara's vernacular. My aging body tends to cramp up if I sit more than a few minutes in any one position, and shifting around only increases the pressure on my tailbone. I had to get out twice and take short walks in the cold wind to stretch the kinks out of my lower back.

Eight-thirty, nine o'clock. A few cars arrived and parked on the street or pulled into the nearside driveway, and half a dozen people went in through the front entrance. None of them was Vinson or Erskine.

Hunger pangs increased my discomfort. I hadn't eaten since

a light lunch. In the old days I kept a bunch of light snacks—potato chips, peanut butter crackers, cookies—in the car for unplanned-for downtime such as this, but now that I did little fieldwork and had pretty much given up junk food for health reasons, I no longer bothered to stock up. All I found when I rummaged around in the glove box was one of the dinky little energy bars Emily is fond of. Apricot, except it didn't taste much like apricot; it tasted like chewy cardboard and only made me hungrier.

Nine-thirty.

Quarter of ten.

The hell with it. It had been a long day, I was tired and stiff and cold as well as hungry, and it was a forty-some-mile drive back to the city. No sense in pushing myself past a sensible limit. Start fresh tomorrow.

I got the engine going and headed for home.

16

But home was not where I went. I took an impulsive and ill-advised detour instead.

I was on Page Mill Road, nearing the intersection with Highway 280, when the thought began to nag at me that Erskine might have taken Vinson home with him. Would the son of a bitch be that bold, that callous? Sure he would. Dinner first, maybe, someplace where they weren't known, then a return to the scene of the crime to finish up their celebration. No risk to him; he'd committed the perfect murder, hadn't he? It wasn't likely any of the neighbors would notice them arriving, but if they were spotted and the fact was later mentioned to him, why, he'd just say she was helping put his wife's affairs in order, or comforting him in his time of need. He wouldn't give much of a damn what the neighbors thought anyway.

Couldn't hurt to swing by his house, could it? It was more or less on the way, a round-trip detour off 280 of only a few miles. If the place was dark I needn't stop; if it showed lights I could ring the bell, late as it was, and see if I could get him to let me in—feed him a story about being on my way back from San Jose, where I'd uncovered some information about the

Leno brothers. Might just work. Then what I could do was make it plain, without actually accusing him, that I had the entire scheme figured. Escalate the war of nerves—the Javert treatment. If Vinson was there and stashed someplace where she could listen to the conversation, it might scare her enough so she'd be easier to crack when I tackled her alone.

It was not much of an idea, a product of weariness, frustration, and a compulsive need to confront Erskine, but I could not talk myself out of it. When the Atherton exit came up, I turned off and let the disembodied voice guide me through a series of curves and turns to the Erskine property.

No lights showed at the front of the house, but the gates at the foot of the drive were wide open. Funny. Whether he was home or not, why hadn't he bothered to close them?

I turned in between them for a better view. Amber-colored ground lanterns illuminated the driveway; more of the same glowed like stationary fireflies all across the grounds. l couldn't tell from here whether or not there were any lit windows at the sides or rear of the house. Except for the night-lights, the darkness was thick with restless shadows. Overhead, fast-moving clouds driven by high-altitude winds hid the stars and the sickle moon except for brief breaks in the leaden canopy.

Well?

Well, I'd come this far. Go on up and ring the bell and let's see what happens.

I drove through the gates and up the drive. Halfway along, where the shrubbery thinned out, I could see part of the lantern-lit path that led to the summerhouse, a darkened hulk against the screen of evergreens. A faint yellowish sheen lay over a portion of the side terrace: drapes open in the sunroom, one or more lights burning inside.

A light-colored Corvette drawn up on the white-pebble parking area confirmed that at least Erskine was here. I rolled up next to it, doused the headlamps. When I got out, I stepped over to the Corvette and laid a hand on its hood. Warm. Wherever he'd been tonight, he hadn't been home long.

I crossed slowly to the porch. The night's silence was broken only by wind-rattle in trees and shrubbery; there were no sounds that I could make out inside the house. If Vinson was here with him, they were somewhere at the rear—in bed together, like as not.

I put my finger on the bell, but I didn't push it. There was tension in me all of a sudden; the skin across my neck and shoulders had begun to pull and prickle. Another of those sixth-sense feelings of wrongness, sudden this time, setting off the silent danger alarm inside my head.

For some seconds I stood still, listening, looking around. Still quiet inside the house, nothing visibly or aurally changed out here. But the feeling remained strong just the same. Strong enough to prod me off the porch, over onto a lit path that led around on the terraced side.

I hadn't gone more than a few steps when the woman screamed.

The cry came from outside the house, toward the rear—a high-pitched shriek that shattered the stillness and brought me up short, raised the hairs on the back of my neck.

Confusion of sounds then: garbled yells, scrapings and scufflings, a sharp metallic clatter as of a wrought-iron table or chair knocked over onto the terrace bricks. The woman screeched again, terrified words this time that carried distinctly on the wind.

"Peter, who . . . oh, God, this can't be happening!"

Another scraping noise, the pop of shattering glass.

The woman: "What're you doing? Why are you—? No! *No, don't—!*"

Running footfalls. And then the sudden crack of a gun, a large-caliber weapon that sent echoes hammering through the darkness.

I had taken a couple of steps toward the corner; the report twisted me around, sent me running back to the car. Only a damn fool rushes unarmed into an unknown, firearms-deadly situation. I dragged the car door open, leaned in to release the hidden compartment under the dash, yanked out the snub-nosed Colt Bodyguard I keep in there for emergencies, and ran back toward the far side of the house.

More sounds battered the night, a male voice now, yelling something I couldn't understand.

Near the corner I slowed, holding the .38 up next to my ear, drawing in close to the sweet-smelling shrubbery that grew there; charge out into the open and you're a target even on a dark night. Before I could get my head around for a clear look, the yelling morphed into a kind of panicked wail. Other cries followed it, diminishing. Man on the run, howling like a banshee.

I stepped out away from the shrubbery with the revolver leveled. A rent in the cloud cover opened just then, letting enough starlight and moonshine leak through to bathe the yard in faint luminescence. In the two or three beats before the tear closed, I had a glimpse of what seemed to be two figures stumbling up the steps into the summerhouse, one clinging to the other from behind. False impression, my old eyes playing tricks. Only one figure had fused into the black-dark inside—Erskine, still emitting that half-crazed wail.

The night was shadow haunted again as I ran in a crouch toward the side terrace. I did not see the woman until I was only a few feet from where she lay in a dip in the lawn beyond the bricks, facedown with both arms outflung.

I veered that way, dropped to one knee beside her—and my stomach churned even though I was braced for the worst. The slug from the shot I'd heard had opened up the back of her head just above the neck; spatters of blood and bone and brain matter matted her black hair. Melanie Vinson. I did not need to touch her to verify it.

Over in the summerhouse, the wailing stopped and Erskine's voice bellowed, "You can't force me this time, I won't let you! Go back where you came from, go to hell!" Then the gun banged loud again.

I ducked instinctively, but the round hadn't been directed my way. Almost immediately, there was another outburst from Erskine in the summerhouse darkness, rising above the noises made by the wind. "Not me, goddamn you, not me, not me!"

The cries were soaked in such visceral terror they drove me up onto my feet, sideways to the path that led over there. Erskine spewed something else, but the wind gusted just then and tore away the sense of it. The wildly flailing tree branches and running clouds created a gyrating dance of shadows, surreal, like images in a madman's dream.

The gun went off a third time.

I was looking straight at the summerhouse and I saw the muzzle flash, saw the shape of him as he went down. An instant later, I saw something else, or thought I did—a different kind of flare, so brief it was like a subliminal image of a comet's tail streaking across the night sky. Gone in an eyeblink, if it had ever been there in the first place.

I stepped farther away from the path, to keep out of the amber glow from the lanterns. But nothing else happened. Silence, now, inside the summerhouse. The only sounds anywhere were the whistles and moans of the wind and the rattling tree branches.

I kept on going, slow, getting the pencil flash out of my pocket with my left hand as I went. At the summerhouse steps I paused again to listen—still nothing to hear—and then climbed them carefully with the .38 extended.

Needless precaution. What was left of Peter Erskine lay on the floor next to one of the chaise lounges, his head as much a bloody mess as Melanie Vinson's, the weapon he'd used, a .357 Magnum, clutched in one hand. The pencil light showed something else, too: scratches on his neck and back, rips in his shirt in half a dozen places.

And no one else was there.

17

The official police verdict, based on what I'd witnessed that night and on the evidence corroborating my suspicions about Marian Erskine's fatal coronary, was murder-suicide. Of course.

That was my verdict, too. Of course.

Peter Erskine had had a psychotic break, brought on by factors that could only be guessed at: fear of punishment for the murder of his wife, uncontrollable rage against his co-conspirator, an unstable psychological makeup. He'd killed Melanie Vinson because she wanted more money, or had threatened him in some way, or for no rational reason at all— love and lust flaring into sudden hatred, sudden violence. Then he'd cracked up completely, run screaming to the summer-house, and blown himself away on the second try.

He'd been the only one in there, all three bullets fired had come from his Magnum, and the only fingerprints found on the weapon were his. It was inconceivable that another person could have been on the property, chased him after he shot the woman, dodged the first bullet, taken the weapon away and used it on Erskine, then escaped without my seeing any sign of

270 • Bill Pronzini

him. The figure that had seemed to be clinging to Erskine was simply a distortion of shadows created by the scudding clouds and the wind-tossed evergreens. The torn shirt and the scratches on his back and neck had been done by Melanie Vinson during the struggle I'd heard on the terrace. The first shot from inside the summerhouse had been aimed at himself, only he'd been in such a state he'd missed completely; that slug had been found lodged in one of the support posts. And the words I'd heard him shouting were nothing more than deranged babblings.

The other explanation that crawled into my head, the supernatural one, I dismissed immediately as absurd. And did not mention to anybody, not even Tamara and Jake Runyon. Antanas Vok's spirit had returned after all to exact vengeance by means of assault and demonic possession? Erskine's blatant, contemptuous mockery of the powers of darkness had provoked sufficient wrath to permit it to happen? No. *Hell*, no. The only demons at work that night were the ones that existed inside Peter Erskine's psyche.

Never mind that a ruthless control freak who had put together a murder plan requiring cold, steel-nerved calculation is about as unlikely a candidate for mental breakdown and willful self-destruction as there is. Never mind that he believed he'd gotten away with it, and therefore had fifteen million reasons to maintain his emotional balance and to go on living. Never mind that the bullet in the support post had been at belt level, opposite where he'd been standing, as if he had fired not at himself but at someone or something in front of him. Never mind that neither skin nor blood had been found under Melanie Vinson's fingernails. And never mind the subliminal flare I thought I'd seen just after the second shot in the summerhouse; it was either my imagination or a retinal anomaly, an afterimage of the gun flash. There are always inconsistencies, unanswerable questions in cases like this. People go off the deep end all the time, for no clear-cut reasons. I'd seen it happen before, on more than one occasion.

Murder-suicide, period.

Because I can't, I won't, believe the dead can harm the living in any way for any purpose.

Because there is no such thing as a revenant.